PUA'S KISS

LAUELE FRACTURED FOLKTALES #1

LEHUA PARKER

MAKENA PRESS

For mana wahine who never trade freedom
for the illusion of a happy ending.

PUA

I t's the sarong's fault.

Lying forgotten in the sand, it beckons to Pua-O-Ke-Kai like a bad wingman carrying too many piña coladas and not enough bail money. It's just a fringed strip of tropical flowers on a bright yellow background, a cheap souvenir destined to be worn for a week in Waikiki and later forgotten in the back of a drawer.

But even a sarong has dreams.

Big dreams.

As the great Niuhi shark Pua-O-Ke-Kai cruises along the reef, the sarong's siren call brings her to the beach like blood in the water.

She can't resist.

At least that's the lie Pua tells herself as she wades out of the ocean and wraps the sarong around her human form.

A glance up and down Keikikai Beach confirms what her Niuhi shark nose already told her: it's deserted. There's just one lone boogie boarder beyond the lava outcrop, out past Piko Point on the Nalupuki beach side.

Nili-boy, she thinks, wiggling her toes in the sand. *A born waterman, but his mother will be angry if she finds out he's surfing alone. Too bad he's much too young to be interesting.*

Raising her face to the sun, she smiles and stretches her arms wide, joints and sinews snapping and popping in ways foreign to a shark. She breathes deeply, giddy as the quick hit of oxygen buzzes her brain.

It's been a long, long time since I've stood on this beach in the daylight. I deserve to warm my bones in the sun. No harm in that.

Curled like a kitten on the sand, she tucks her arm beneath her head and closes her eyes.

Just for a minute.

Funny how easily destiny makes you her bitch.

JUSTIN

Fiddling with the car's radio, I can't find anything but static and one station playing luau music. It's too much in this heat. I flick it off and face the grim reality.

I'm lost.

From Waikiki, it can't be this far to Lauele. The island's not that big. For the millionth time, I check the map and run my finger along the narrow two-lane road hugging the coast, looking for the tiny red x the rental agent drew.

Did the last road sign say Kaimuki? I think so. No, that can't be. According to the map, Kaimuki isn't near the ocean, and I'm definitely following the coast. It was K-something.

Kapolei?

Keawaula?

Kahuku?

Ka'a'awa?

Crap. Nothing makes sense. Hawaiian place names

are all Ks or Hs with too many vowels. Give me a simple name I can find on a map. San Diego. Anaheim. La Jolla, even.

I peer through the windshield looking for the sun, but it's behind clouds. I can't tell if I'm heading west or south. Everything's palm trees, blue ocean, white sand, and towering green cliffs.

Probably circled the island at least twice by now.

I've been driving for days.

Or maybe just two or three hours. Nothing's normal anymore. It hasn't been for a very long time.

This is getting ridiculous. How hard can it be to visit the town my family came from?

When did I last see a sign that was more than a posted speed limit? The only car on the road in the last five miles passed me going the other way.

No stores or gas stations in sight.

Tank's half full, at least. Thank goodness for small favors.

Keeping one eye on the road, I spread the map over the steering wheel. Oahu is littered with towns along the coast, but I'm surrounded by endless jungle on one side and ocean on the other. Beyond this two-lane highway and the occasional power line in the distance, there are no signs of civilization.

In the heat, I shiver.

No wonder Mom's family left Lauele for California and never came back.

They couldn't find it again.

I take a deep breath.

Relax, dumbass. It's an island. As long as I keep heading in one direction, the worst that can happen is I'm right back where I started.

Tossing the map, I wince as the car's vinyl seats tear at my skin like an aesthetician's wax strip.

This sucks.

I need to grab a beach towel from the trunk to sit on, maybe put a tee-shirt over the back of the bucket seat.

I've seen locals in beach cars.

I'd blend.

At the Aloha Island Rentals counter at the airport, downgrading to a car with no AC didn't seem like a big deal, but driving with the windows down is like riding in hell's hairdryer.

A glance in the rearview mirror tells me all I need to know. If I don't want to scare small children or get mistaken for a homeless dude, I'd better pick up a hat.

In a convertible, wind in your hair is sexy.

In this pregnant roller skate, it's just pathetic.

Sasha would never have been caught dead in a car like this.

Sasha.

Just thinking her name is enough to evoke her.

Conjured from my mind like a bad dream, Sasha pops into the empty passenger's seat. She turns to me and says, "That's the difference between you and me, Justin. I always go first-class. No regrets." She tips her head to the side and pouts, the red of her lipstick matching her manicured fingers and toes.

It's a look I know well, a look that says *my way*. With Sasha, there is no *else*, no *highway*, no possibility of any other way but her way existing in the entire universe.

I grind my teeth.

I'm not taking the bait.

She sighs, and it's the sound of a martyr burdened

with the terminally stupid. "But you couldn't even get that right."

I shake my head. I don't want to continue our imaginary conversation, but I do. Now that she's gone, I say all the things I should've said to her face.

Sasha, it's your fault that I booked us a luxury, non-refundable honeymoon package. You always go first-class? Right. Try picking up the check for once and see how long that lasts. This whole trip is use it or lose it, and it's all on me and my credit cards. Thanks for that. At least the guy at Aloha Island Rentals did me a solid by allowing me to switch the Mercedes convertible you reserved for this P.O.S. and refunding the difference. Maybe now I can eat more than ramen and tortillas next month. Hope you and that bastard Palo rot in hell.

Sasha pulls down her Maui Jim sunglasses so I can see her roll her eyes. "Palo is a godsend. He taught me who I really am."

I know exactly who you are. You're Sasha Maria Rodriguez. We were together for five years, five happy years, until you got starry-eyed planning our extravagant fairy tale wedding, dumped me at the altar, and married our wedding planner instead.

"Don't be mad. I just swapped the Pauper for the Prince."

Prince? You mean the guy pushing discounted floral arrangements and cheap cover bands? That's what you wanted?

"And what did you want, Justin? More art supplies?"

I wanted to get married, Sasha. I promised you I'd make

you happy, and I always keep my promises. You're the one who broke faith.

She pushes her glasses back into place with a sigh. "It never would've worked, Justin. Like Palo says, I've evolved beyond you."

Palo's a pretentious prick who thinks people prefer lemon-thyme cake with tomato confit over chocolate. That's not evolved. That's Pinterest.

"Don't be angry. You would've tried and tried to make us work because that's who you are, Justin, but you could never satisfy my needs. Can't you be happy I've found someone who can?"

You sure about that, chica? No matter what you say, there's no way Fabulous Palo with the color-coded binders, bleached tips, and appetizers to die for doesn't play for both teams.

"Sticks and stones, Justin. True love—"

True love, my left—

The road curves sharper than I expect, and I take the corner too fast.

Oh—

Tires squeal. The hotel's complimentary bottle of Dom Perignon tips and rolls against the passenger door. Heart thumping, I fight to keep four tires on the pavement and my P.O.S. car in my lane.

It's a near thing; there's more rubber on the road now than on my tires. I slow it down and breathe.

Without missing a beat, Sasha points to the bottle and says, "Where's the card?"

We almost died, Sasha.

She shrugs. "Not me. I'm only in your head. Where's the card that said Welcome Mr. & Mrs.

Halpert?" She sniffs. "Did you keep it for your scrapbook?"

Pleeze. That's too catty even for you.

"But you kept the champagne." She puts her hand to her chest and pretends to look around. "No crystal flutes?"

No need for a glass when there's one set of lips, Sasha.

"A whole bottle of honeymoon champagne for yourself? Aw, that's so sad."

I'm not going to waste a drop. Not going to waste this trip either.

I wipe the sweat out of my eyes, refusing to look at her any longer.

Done.

I'm so done.

Done before I started.

I wiggle in my seat, eyes darting to the center console with the empty Super Big Gulp in the cup holder.

It's hot. No AC. Can't drink champagne and drive, so I stopped at a convenience store. What can I say?

I even ate the ice.

Don't think about the pressure threatening to erupt.

I'm just going to swallow hard and ignore how the ocean crashes against the shore. I'm not thinking about how much this seat belt pushes against my bladder.

Oh, man.

Please, God. Don't make me be the guy who pulls off the side of the road to pee in the bushes like a three-year-old on a family trip. And if I really have to be that guy, please don't let me be the guy who also gets arrested for indecent exposure.

On his honeymoon.

Alone.

Sasha snickers. "Loser," she says.

Ugh! It's been a week. Get out of my head!

She blows me a kiss. "Don't worry, Justin. I'll still visit you in prison."

The vein in my temple bulges.

That's—

No, no, no. Bad idea. Bad. Don't get angry. Relax. Anger makes gut muscles clench.

Sensing weakness, Sasha goes for the kill. She rises from the passenger's seat to float in front of my face, banging a tin cup against prison bars.

"Look on the bright side. In addition to three hot meals a day, you'll finally get to use your fancy art degree to create prison tats."

Ka-BOOM.

I'm swearing so hard, I almost miss it: the big beach pavilion and public restrooms across the street from a store called Hari's.

Hallelujah! Saved.

I screech into the parking lot, peel my body from the vinyl seat, and sprint past the sign saying Keikikai Beach.

Another Hawaiian K place. What a surprise.

Standing at the urinal, the relief is immediate. I start to grin.

Sorry, Sasha. No prison cobweb or teardrop tatts today.

But if I did them, they'd rock.

Washing my hands, I catch myself in the mirror: stubble-streaked chin, red eyes, wild hair.

Crazy.

Or homeless.

I lean close and narrow my eyes.

Not crazy. Not homeless.

Dangerous.

I turn the water off and run my wet hands through my hair, sweeping it back and to the side.

Better. Less psycho, more Wall Street.

It hits me.

I can be different.

I don't have to be the guy who flies with an empty seat beside him in first-class. I can be the guy who finds a young couple flying coach and trades seats.

I don't have to be the guy who gets lost circling an island because staying alone in the honeymoon suite is just too hard.

And I definitely don't have to be the guy who allows the memory of his former fiancé to torment him with his own insecurities.

I can be New Me.

It's only afternoon, I have a bottle of warm bubbly all to myself, and I no longer give a damn.

Not going to prison.

Yet.

3

JUSTIN

Coming out of the bathroom, I walk to the edge of the pavilion and survey the beach below. It's a wide bay split by an outcrop of lava dotted with tide pools. The beach in front of me is calm and shallow, the water clear all the way to the sandy bottom. On the far side of the lava outcrop, the ocean is darker and wilder, hinting at deep water. I bet when conditions are right, the surfing's good over there.

Sunlight tickles the water as clouds reflect in tide pools. Patterns lie just beneath the surface. I feel a familiar twitch between my shoulder blades as my mind takes the shapes, the dark and the light, and twists them.

I flex my fingers, considering.

Behind me are picnic tables and benches. The pavilion sits on a rise above the beach. The breeze off the ocean is fresh and clean.

New Me says, "Seize the moment. Drive to Lauele another day."

He's right. It's time to create.

Back at the car, I get my sketch pad and a pencil. They're nothing fancy, but I keep them with me for times when memory alone isn't enough to capture what I'm seeing.

What I'm feeling.

As I lock the car, the bottle catches my eye. Picking it up, I know Sasha's right. Drinking honeymoon champagne alone is beyond sad.

New Me says, "Take it back and leave it for house-keeping."

I sigh.

There better be extra chocolates on my pillow if I do.

But before I can put the bottle back, a muse whispers in my ear. "Forget housekeeping. Sunset's only a couple of hours away. As the sun slips beyond the horizon, open the bottle on the beach, take a sip, and pour the rest into the ocean in honor of broken-hearted homies everywhere."

Beautiful! I'll do it.

"And then forget that wench, pick your lame ass off the ground, and never look back."

Whoa. Cranky muse.

But she's right.

Tomorrow's a new day.

A new Sasha-less day.

I'm gonna be New Me.

Now let's all hold hands and sing *Kumbaya.*

New Me shakes my head.

Maybe not.

Crossing the pavilion, I place the bottle on a picnic

table and perch beside it. Flipping to a blank page, I lose myself in art.

Half-way through the sketch, I'm ambushed.

"Eh, excuse, yeah? You know what time the Waimanalo bus come?"

"Holy—!" Startled, my pencil jerks across the page and strikes the bottom of a walking boogie board.

"Eh, watch it! No ding my board!" The board shifts to reveal a boy's shock of surfer-white hair, fierce brown eyes, and a puka shell necklace. He checks the back of his board and scowls, licking his thumb to swipe at the pencil mark.

I look down at my sketch pad. There's a bold line that doesn't belong. No way that's going to erase as easily as the mark on the boogie board.

Ruined.

I'll have to start over.

Perfect.

I sigh.

The boy says, "Eh, brah, you lucky it only scratched!"

"Sorry. You startled me."

Mid-scrub, his eyes narrow. He raises an eyebrow and cocks his head to the side. "What you said?"

"I said I'm sorry about your board." I turn my sketch pad toward him. "If it makes you feel better, my drawing's trashed."

His shoulders sag. "You're not from around here."

I throw my hands up and laugh. "I don't even know where here is."

He spots the bottle and tips his chin. "You lolo or drunk?"

"I don't know what lolo is, but the cork's still in the bottle."

The boy cranes his neck and sees that the bottle is unopened. "Huh," he says, "not drunk, so you must be lolo, then. Only crazy people don't know where they are."

I smile. "Not crazy. Lost."

"Fo'real?" He looks around, waving an arm. "This is the pavilion above Keikikai Beach. There's a sign out front and everything."

"I was trying to find Lauele Town," I say.

"Lauele?" He wrinkles his nose.

I shrug. "It's complicated."

He shakes his head. "No, it's not, brah. This beach is in Lauele."

"Really?" I turn toward the road. "Where's the town?"

The boy throws his arm wide and spins in a half-circle. "This whole place is Lauele. Hari's store is across the street. Nalupuki beach is over there. Aunty Liz-dem's house is that way. Lauele Elementary is mauka—toward the mountains. The boat harbor is a couple miles, maybe, but still in Lauele. What you trying fo' find?"

I rub my eyes. No wonder it's not on the map. Lauele isn't a town, it's a wide spot in the road.

"Nothing," I say, pinching the bridge of my nose. "I just wanted to see it. My family came from here."

"Oh, so you're a Coconut," he says, shuffling his feet and rocking his board. "Shoulda known."

"What?"

He has the grace to blush just a little bit, but won't meet my eyes.

He mumbles, "When I first saw you, I thought for sure you were from around here. You were sitting on top the table like a local braddah. Your hair is dark. You're wearing surfer shorts. But when I get closer, I see you drawing, drawing, drawing, paying no attention to anything else. And then I see you're wearing shoes and socks AT THE BEACH! Ho, that's one classic Coconut move. Shoulda known you not going know nothing about buses."

"Coconuts don't ride buses?"

"Coconuts drive rentals."

"And wear shoes and socks to the beach? That's a Coconut?" I ask.

The boy flaps his hand. "Brah, Coconuts are brown on the outside, white on the inside. That's you. You look like a local, but you're not."

I eye the boy's golden tan and spiky blond hair. He's no pure-blooded Hawaiian, either.

"So, if I'm a Coconut, what are you?"

"Me?" The boy proudly squares his shoulders. "I'm a Cocoa Puff!"

I blink. "A what?"

"A Cocoa Puff! You know, a malasada with choco-late dobash filling." When I don't respond, he smacks his forehead. "It's like a chocolate-filled doughnut. Golden delicious on the outside, brown on the inside."

"I see," I say, and bite my lip.

"Eh, no laugh! All the wahines love Cocoa Puffs!"

"Wahines? Girls, you mean? How old are you?"

"Nine. Why, how old are you?"

"Old enough."

"For what?"

"To know what women really want," I say.

The boy tips his head to the side. "Uh huh. That's why you're sitting here all by yourself with a full bottle of wine?"

"Maybe I'm meeting someone."

The boy nods sagely. "Truth," he says, "but if you're going to share that bottle, you better get some glasses. Wahines don't like germs. Girls are funny kine li'dat."

"Thanks for the tip."

"No prob. So, Cuz, you for sure don't know when the next bus coming?"

"Nope. Sorry."

"Shoots. My mom's gonna be cock-a-roach-killing, slippah-mad when I'm not home before sunset." He shakes his head and looks at his feet. "An'den," he sighs.

"Anden? That's your name?"

"No, brah. Wow. You look local, but you're such a Coconut, like fo'reals."

I'm not entirely sure what he's saying. I flip my sketch pad closed, tuck my pencil behind my ear, and stand.

"So, you're good?" I say, grabbing the bottle. "You need bus money?"

"No. Thanks, but." The boy picks up his boogie board and shifted uneasily.

"What?" I ask.

He opens his mouth, then snaps it shut.

"What?"

He presses his lips tight and shrugs.

"You already called me a Coconut. It's all good," I say. "Just tell me. I can take it."

"Eh, you're not going swimming, right?" he blurts.

I look at him nonplussed. "It's a beach."

"Yeah, but…" He points to a sign near the showers.

Danger. Shark zone. Swim at your own risk. At the bottom is a picture of a swimmer one second from being a Jaws snack.

At first glance, it's hilarious. I've seen signs like this posted by locals in California to scare tourists away. Keikikai must be a locals only beach.

And then I get pissed.

I reach out and thump the back of his boogie board. His eyes go wide, and he flinches a little as I loom over him.

"Didn't you just come out of the water?" I say.

"Yeah," he says slowly, puzzled by my tone. "But it's different for me."

I stand tall, cross my arms, and look down my nose. "Sharks don't bite Cream Puffs?"

"Cocoa Puffs!"

"Right, Cocoa Puffs. Sharks don't bite you because you're a Cocoa Puff?"

He looks down, confused. After a beat he mutters, "Something li'dat."

I waver. There's more going on here; he's genuinely concerned for me. I relax my arms and shift my weight.

I say, "You aren't afraid of sharks."

His chin snaps up. "Only stupid heads not afraid of sharks," he spits.

I think for a second. "You aren't afraid of sharks *here*."

"No, but—"

"Have you seen sharks here?" I press.

He swallows and looks away for a second, then decides. "Yeah," he says. "I seen sharks here." He points to the end of the lava outcrop. "That's Piko Point." He sweeps his arm to the right. "That beach is Nalupuki. Good surfing right off Piko Point. On your board, if you look down in the water there, you'll see choke reef sharks—black tip, grey reef, sandbar—"

I interrupt. "Not all sharks are dangerous."

He flashes me a relieved look. "Right! Those kinds of sharks you don't worry about. You just keep an eye on them. If they start acting funny, that's your warning to get out of the water."

"Got it. So why does the sign show a big shark about to eat someone?"

He points to the ocean beyond the lava outcrop. "Out there are other sharks—big sharks. Niuhi sharks. Unlike a reef shark, you can't just look down into the water to see if they're annoyed. You never see Niuhi sharks coming unless they want you to see them."

"Sharks are ambush predators. Why would a shark want me to see him?"

He blinks, surprised. "To make a point about something. To make sure you understand that they're the boss. You never want a Niuhi shark *interested*, you know, curious about you. If they mark you, you might as well say your good-byes because you're already make-die dead and just don't know it." He meets my eyes. "Fo'real," he says. "No joke. If a Niuhi shark marks you, you're never safe. You're shark bait every time."

"The sign's not a joke? There really are big sharks out there?"

"Yeah."

"Can you show me?"

He shakes his head. "Not now."

"You were surfing five minutes ago. What's changed?"

He points to the sun two finger widths away from kissing the water.

"Sunset, brah. You don't want to believe me, fine. But never go into the ocean at night, especially around Lauele. Anybody'll tell you that."

"Okay. No swimming tonight. Just walking, promise."

The boy's shoulders ease.

"But honestly, I'm coming back tomorrow. I'd like to see some sharks."

"You sure? Maybe it's better if you stay in Waikiki. No sharks," he says.

"But more people."

"Truth. But that's why no sharks."

"I like sharks."

He dusts a bit of sand from his elbow and sighs. "You're one stupid head Coconut, for sure. Nobody likes sharks."

He leans his board against the table and walks to a spindly plant growing near the parking lot.

"If you're going to get in the water, you better know how to stay safe." He touches a leaf. "It's called a ki plant. Take some leaves and twist them into a lei to wear in the ocean." He holds out his leg so I can see the intricately braided ki leaf lei around his ankle. "Like this."

"Nice," I say.

"Here, you try." He breaks off a couple of leaves and hands them to me. In my palms, I roll them against each other. They're waxy and slender, like leaves on corn stalks. I lift them to my nose, but I don't smell anything special.

The boy clicks his tongue. "Never mind. I'll make it." Snatching the leaves back, he deftly shreds them into strips, weaves a simple braid, and presents the finished lei. "Of course, mine's more fancy, but that'll work."

"That's shark repellant? A braided leaf?"

"Underwater, all legs look the same. That lei marks you as a local and asks the Niuhi sharks not to bite. I mean, they'll still bite if they want to, but the lei just reminds everyone to be a good neighbors."

"Oh. Makes perfect sense."

He looks at me, unsure if I'm making fun.

At this point, I'm not sure either.

"My mom says you don't need wear the lei in a specific place, but I put mine on my ankle 'cause I figure when you're sitting on a surfboard, sharks can't see a lei around your neck. Legs always dangle, yeah?"

"Smart."

He walks back to his board and gives me a little wave. "Okay, then. If you see a big shark out there—"

"—get out of the water."

His brown eyes turn serious. "You can't. By then it's too late. But you can always try to tell them you're friends with Nili-boy. It might help."

"Who's Nili-boy?"

"That's me."

"Of course it is."

Nili-boy lifts his board and balances it on his head. "Laters, Coconut." He flashes me a hand signal, thumb and pinkie extended, middle three fingers folded against his palm.

Shark sign language, I'm sure.

And he thought *I* was crazy.

"Bye, Nili-boy," I say. "Thanks for the lei. But what if I meet a tourist shark, and he doesn't know you?"

"Pray, brah. That's all you got left." He tips his chin toward the lei in my hand. "Better put it on now before you forget."

"I won't. I'm not going to forget any of this."

Shaking his head and muttering about coconuts, sunsets, and bus stops, I watch as Nili-boy carries his boogie board down the street and out of sight.

I read the sign again and snort.

Shark zone.

Right.

I put the ki leaf lei in my back pocket before slipping off my shoes and socks and leaving them on the rock wall near the sign. As I head down to the water, the sand burns, so I step a little quicker.

Cooling my feet at the ocean's edge, I watch how the colors melt from clear turquoise at the shore to deep purple at the horizon, so different from the uniform gray of the California coast. The breeze off the water is refreshing, not freezing, and smells like salted flowers and sunshine.

Maybe if I lived here, I wouldn't want to share, either.

I tuck my sketchbook under my arm and turn my attention to the bottle. Stripping the foil, I slip it into my pocket before popping the cork. Angry champagne froths down my arm. Warm and shaken too much, it's eager to merge with the sea-foam at my feet and be done.

"To Sasha," I say, and tip the bottle to my lips. My mouth fills with sparkling air and the faint taste of sour grapes. The bubbles roll up the back of my nose, making my sinuses burn.

What a whole lot of nothing.

I turn the bottle over and pour the rest into the sea.

4

JUSTIN

I walk.

Maybe it's to find shells. Maybe it's just to move a little before the long drive back to Waikiki. Maybe it's to finish becoming New Me.

Maybe it's fate.

All I know is one minute I'm walking along the beach at the sweet spot where the sand is firm and the ocean gently kisses your toes, and the next I'm noticing a bright spot of color against the white sand.

Someone's beach towel or mat?

Mildly curious, I look out to sea and along the beach, but there's no one around. Moving closer, a shape takes form—a dark head and curled legs.

Is that a body?

Heart pumping faster, I start to jog, watching for movement, for breathing, for anything to tell me to hurry or slow down. My hand reaches for my cell phone in my pocket.

911, right? Even in Hawaii it's got to be 911.

Closer now, I see it's a woman lying on the sand, wrapped in a bright yellow sarong.

Do people do that, just lie in the sand without a beach mat?

Is she hurt?

No blood.

Her hair is dark and her skin, copper. She looks local. Maybe islanders don't bother with beach mats.

When I get close enough to see her chest gently rise, I slow.

I pause a few feet from her.

Not dead.

Sleeping.

The setting sun is soft on her features. With her knees drawn up, ankles crossed, and her arm cradling her head, there's an air of innocence about her. Long lashes sweep high cheekbones; her nose is straight and narrow; her full lips rest in a Mona Lisa smile.

Like a sea nymph come ashore.

I squat, tipping my head this way and that, mesmerized by the way light moves over her, the way the breeze toys with bits of loose hair, the way small specks of sand cling to her cheeks. My fingers twitch with the need to paint, to capture this moment forever. I sink to the sand, pull my pencil from behind my ear, and start to sketch.

One sweep of a soft line to suggest her arm tucked behind her head. Another line forms the shape of her face—forehead, nose, eyes, lips, chin. A shadow creates the hollow in her throat. Stroke, smudge, slide —my pencil moves without thought as my eyes devour her.

The pink and gold of the sunset dances in her hair—
Argh! I can't capture it with this black pencil! Her eyes are—

Her eyes are—

Her eyes are looking right at me.

Oh, crap. I'm THAT guy.

I'm sitting on the beach next to a beautiful woman, a stranger, practically drooling.

She blinks once, twice.

She opens her mouth.

I brace myself for the scream.

"Hi," she says with a sigh. She sits up and sweeps a stray bit of hair away from her face. "That was glorious."

What the what? Is she for real?

"What's wrong?" she says. "You look like you've seen a ghost."

"N...n...nothing's wrong. Sorry to disturb you." I snap my book closed, tuck my pencil behind my ear, and scramble to get up.

She tips her head to the side. "Are you sure? You look pale around the lips. You aren't going to faint on me, are you?"

Light-headed, I sit back down. "I don't think so. I was actually worried about you."

"Me?"

"I thought you might be dead."

She smiles. "How sweet. That's the nicest thing anyone's said to me in a long time."

I puff out my cheeks in disbelief. "I said I thought you were dead!"

"I heard you. You were worried. That means you care. I bet you're honest and trustworthy, too."

"You make me sound like a Boy Scout," I say.

"Is that a bad thing?"

"Well—"

"See? You can't even lie about that," she says, idly brushing sand off her shoulders.

"You don't mind the sand?" I blurt.

"What's to mind?"

I open my mouth and shut it again.

Did I just fall down a rabbit hole?

I shake my head and start again.

"So, you're okay?"

"I'm fine, but as I recall, we started this conversation wondering about your health." She raises an eyebrow.

"Well, I'm fine, too."

"Great."

"Great."

We look at each other.

"Okay, then." I stand. "Guess I'd better be going."

She raises her arms over her head and stretches with the grace of ballet dancer, her breasts straining against the sarong.

Is the knot going to hold?

I can't breathe.

"Going where?" she asks.

"What?" I say.

"You said you had to be going. Going where?"

"Back to my hotel," I squeak.

"Waikiki?"

"Yeah."

She grins, and her face lights up like it's Christmas, the 4th of July, and her birthday all at once. "You're not from around here."

"No, I'm from the States."

The corner of her mouth twitches. "Yes, I've heard of it. Pretty big place."

Too late, I realize what I said. "I mean I know Hawaii's a state, I just…um..."

In my head, Sasha laughs. "Smooth as Ex-Lax," she says.

Shut up, Sasha!

"You sure you're all right? You've gone from pale to flushed."

I sit back down.

Up. Down. Up. Down. I'm worse than a bloody Jack-in-the-box.

"I'm sorry," I say. "I'm not very good at this."

"Hello, Not Very Good at This. My name is Pua-O-Ke-Kai."

My mouth stumbles. "Pua-O…"

"Call me Pua, for short. It means flower." She holds out her hand.

I take it. It's soft and warm.

I want to lick it.

I shake my head.

What is wrong with me?

I say, "Hello, Pua For Short. I'm Justin. I have no idea what my name means. My parents chose it."

She laughs. "Mine, too. With this much in common, we're destined to be friends."

"Thank you for not screaming."

"Because we're friends?"

"Because you caught me staring at you like some weirdo while you were sleeping."

"Most women would have screamed?"

"Oh, yeah," I say.

Her eyes widen.

"I mean, it wasn't like that, I'm not a pervert—"

"Good to know," she says.

I stop and take a breath. "I told you I wasn't very good at this."

"You're doing fine. Can I have my hand back?"

"Oh! Sorry!"

"So, if you're not a pervert, what are you?"

"A painter."

"Of houses?"

"Of portraits." I wave my sketch book. "I was trying to visualize how I would paint you."

"Flattery. And you say you're not good at this."

I grin. "I also do some sculpting and ceramics."

"An artist."

"A jack of all trades and a master of none. At least my professors think so."

"Professors? You're a scholar?"

"More like permanent student. I'm on the five-year MFA plan at UCLA. A.B.D."

"A.B.D.?" she asks.

"All But Dissertation. I haven't finished my portfolio for an art show."

"Is that why you're here?"

"It's complicated," I hedge.

"Maybe you'll feel inspired by the islands," she says, toying with her hair. "Many do."

"How about you?"

"Oh, I'm long done with school, but not with learning. The world's too interesting for that."

"I like that," I say. "Out of school, but still a student. So, what do you do with yourself?"

She smiles wider. "I travel."

"Trust fund baby."

"No, but you're right. I don't worry about money."

"Must be nice."

She looks out to sea. "No worries about money, but plenty about time. The sun's gone down. I've got to get going. Kalei's going to be furious if he finds out I've spent the afternoon on the beach."

I knew it. Girls like her are never free.

"Kalei's your boyfriend?"

She stands, brushing sand off her butt.

Butt.

Don't stare at her butt.

Absentmindedly, she shakes sand off the front of her sarong.

I wonder what she's wearing underneath.

Or not wearing.

I squeeze my eyes tight.

Maybe I am a pervert.

She reaches up and pulls her hair into a knot on the top of her head. "Kalei's my brother. I don't have a boyfriend," she says.

Want one? New Me growls.

Stop being a pig.

Bet I could make you forget time, too.

Just. Stop.

I swallow.

Keeping my eyes glued to her face, I say, "Your brother can't be that mad at you. Tell him it was an emergency. A beach emergency. You had to help a tourist out."

She says, "But now that you're okay, and I'm okay…"

"You have to go. I understand."

I stand and brush sand off my shorts, angling my butt toward her just a little bit.

Two can play this game.

Damn.

She's not looking.

Chillax. Just play it cool.

"It's time I headed back, too," I say.

I pause.

Go for it, New Me shouts.

"I'd like to see you again."

Surprised, she steps toward me. "You would?"

"If that's all right?"

"You're sure about this? You're choosing of your own free will to see me again?" Her lips curl inscrutably, like the cat that licked the coconut cream.

I grab my cell phone out of my pocket. "What's your number?"

"I don't have one."

"You don't have one?"

"No."

"Oh. Do you want my phone number?" I ask.

"I don't have a phone."

I look at her. "Do you have a quarter? I can give you one."

"Why?"

"Pay phones. It was a joke."

"Pay phones are funny?" she says.

I sigh. "How are we going to meet again?"

"The usual way," she gestures, "along the beach."

"Along the beach?"

"Uh huh."

"You live around here?" I ask.

"Not far."

"Where?"

She steps close and leans toward me, gently placing her forehead on mine, nose to nose.

What the what? She wants to kiss? Here? Now?

New Me jumps to attention.

Don't wait for an engraved invitation, idiot! Kiss her!

I start to push forward to capture her lips, but she doesn't yield. She places her hands on my shoulders and holds me in place.

She exhales, her breath rising from her lungs to crawl up my nostrils and hover in the back of my throat. The scent of lemon, salt, sandalwood, and something I can't identify swirls around me. I feel light-headed and dizzy like I've downed a shot or ten of tequila on an empty stomach.

I sway, but she holds me steady.

The air rushes out of my lungs, and it's her turn to breathe deeply.

She holds me just a beat longer, then steps back.

What the hell just happened?

I shake my head to clear it.

Crap! I run my tongue over my teeth. When did I last brush?

"I find you *interesting*, Justin. Don't worry," she says, "I'll find you. We carry a part of each other now."

"Pua—"

"Goodbye, Justin. See you soon." She turns and lightly runs toward the lava outcrop that stretches out to sea.

I'm still too dizzy to do more than blink.

Seriously, what the hell was that all about?

Bemused, I watch her tiptoe barefoot over the rocks.

Oh, no. Her shoes.

I search the sand where she was lying, but she's left nothing behind.

When I look back toward the outcrop, she's gone.

What?

I scan the beach, but there's no sign of her.

Can't be. There's nowhere to go.

Did she fall?

I start to jog over, but with the sun over the horizon, it's hard to distinguish the water from the rocks.

A trick of the light. That's it.

I touch my nose, still feeling her forehead against mine.

What was that breathing thing?

Was she flirting with me? It didn't feel like flirting.

Did she want me to kiss her? I should have kissed her.

I'm such an idiot.

I don't see the wave that splashes against my knees.

Tide's coming in.

The usual way.

We'll met again the usual way.

I kick a rotten coconut husk as I turn toward the pavilion.

How many guys does it take for there to be a usual way?

How could she not have a phone?

Was she playing me?

She was playing me. No one that good looking and over 21 worries about what her brother thinks.

Of course she has a boyfriend.

He's probably the one with the trust fund.

I am an idiot.

I shake my head.

Get a grip.

New Me says, "You went from *she's the love of your life* to *she's a tramp* in one breath. Chill. You'll see her if you see her."

I'm such an idiot.

5

PUA

Surrounded by ink-black ocean and cold lava rock, Pua waits for her brother, Kalei. The moon isn't quite full, maybe in another night or two, but it still shines like a beacon over Piko Point. The ocean is calm, the sky clear, and the stars and moon sparkle like jewels in the large saltwater pool near her feet. She sits and toys with small hermit crabs, trying to decide how much she will tell Kalei about Justin, that strange young man who'd caught her napping in the sun.

All tourists are crazy. She should forget Justin and not meet him again, especially here on this beach.

She shouldn't, but she knows she will.

Pua hugs her knees, looking out to sea. She feels her brother Kalei walk up behind her, not because the echo of his slight limp reverberates through the lava—his missing right toe tends to throw-off his gait—but simply because she knows he's there.

Twins always know.

"Pua."

"Kalei." She doesn't turn around.

"You weren't at the harbor this afternoon."

"I'm sorry."

"I waited."

"I lost track of time."

"That's impossible."

She rolls her eyes. "It's the truth."

Kalei sits beside her. His fingers tug the edge of her sarong. "I've never seen this before."

"It's new," she says, eyes back on the sea.

Kalei follows her gaze and sighs. "You're distracted. What's wrong?"

"Nothing."

"I don't believe you."

"It's nothing."

"Your lips are pale. When did you last eat?"

She shrugs.

His eyes narrow. "You've met someone."

She shrugs again, not meeting his eyes.

"Pua? You did, didn't you? It's been decades since I've seen you like this, but I know I'm right. Tell me true." He licks his lips. "Is he delicious?"

She grins. "He is easy on the eyes."

"You naughty girl! You find him *interesting*?"

She nods. "We honi'd. I marked him. He's mine."

"Breath mingles in bodies? So soon! Details!"

"He's a tourist."

"Of course. Tell me something I don't know."

"Young. Mid-twenties. He's an artist from California. I really don't know much about him. He wants to see me again."

"He said that? Before or after the honi?"

"Before."

"How utterly delightful. He's baring his belly. How'd you meet? Waikiki? Is that where you got that ridiculous sarong?"

She fiddles for a moment with the fringe, smoothing it over her knees. "No, I found it on the beach this afternoon." She points to Keikikai in the distance. "Just over there."

Kalei stills, all joking pushed aside. "You walked on Keikikai beach in the daylight?"

"Napped, actually."

He puts his hand over his mouth for a beat, then shakes his head. "I don't have to tell you how dangerous that is."

"No."

"Why, Pua? You know Father's kapu."

"The kapu only says that no Niuhi-human sons may be born. It doesn't forbid napping on the beach in the sun."

"If you want to lie in the sun, go to the northern islands. Visit Aunty Ake at Respite Beach. Head to California or Tahiti for all I care. But you can't lie on the beach in Lauele. It's too dangerous."

"Father's rules."

"The Great Ocean God Kanaloa's *kapu* laws, Pua. You're playing with fire, and you know it. The only way for you to have a son is to mate with a human whose bloodlines come from Lauele—"

"—under a full moon and on the beach at Keikikai. I know, I know. And that's a world away from what happened this afternoon."

"Did anyone see you?"

"Nili-boy was surfing alone at Nalupuki. There wasn't anyone else when I came up the beach."

Kalei waves his hand. "I'm not worried about Nili-boy. But napping in the sun at Keikikai, that's risky behavior even for you."

"I couldn't help it. I was just so tired."

"Tired? Impossible."

"Not tired, exactly. Restless. I came to Keikikai because there was an itchy feeling right beneath my dorsal fin. No matter what I did, I couldn't scratch it. When I spotted the sarong on the shore, I had to have it. I was all the way up the beach before I realized what I had done. But the sun felt so good, Kalei, the air so fresh in my lungs—"

"You had to stay," he says, his tone flat as death.

"Yeah," Pua says.

Kalei leans over and inhales Pua's scent, confirming what he suspects. "You're kahe."

Pua bolts upright. "That's impossible! Father wouldn't allow it."

"He told you to stay away from Lauele. Did you listen?"

"I—"

"Let me see the back of your neck, Pua."

"No."

Kalei snatches her hair and twists.

"Hey!" Pua struggles, slapping at his arms, but he ignores her and lifts the braid off her neck. In the moonlight, the turtle tattoo is faint, but distinct along her nape.

"The turtle mark is there. You're kahe. Your body is ready to bear children."

"I don't believe you."

"It's there, Pua. I wouldn't lie to you about this."

"I'm Niuhi, not a bitch in heat."

Kalei drops her braid and slides his arm around her shoulders. "Think about it. Your maternal instincts are driving you here. Why else would you come to the one place that means death for us all?"

"And whose fault is that? I remember when *you* were kahe, Kalei, and running to Lauele like salmon up a river. I remember Nanaue, the son you had with a human mother, the son who turned into a monster and got us banished from our home."

In the darkness, Kalei flinches. "Nanaue became a monster because his human grandfather wouldn't deny him anything."

Pua's voice drops to a hiss. "Centuries ago, Father promised the villagers we'd never return to Lauele. Their sons and daughters would be safe. No more Niuhi-human children like Nanaue who lure friends into the water and eat them like poi. Banished from our ancestral lands! We have your son to thank for that!"

"Pua—"

"And because of you and your appetites, I can never be a mother. Did you ever think about that? No. All you worry about is your duty to Father and his laws."

Kalei explodes. "And why is that? Do you ever think about what it means to me if you break kapu? I have to kill you, Pua, you and your Niuhi-human son! If I don't—"

"Father kills us all. I know."

"Do you, Pua? Do you understand why I get so angry when you hang around Lauele—in human form, no less?"

"I am in control of my destiny, Kalei. I'm not a mindless rutting goat."

"Are you willing to do what it takes to not conceive, Pua? You're not so fond of red meat as I recall."

"Devour him, you mean? That's only necessary if the man is from Lauele, remember?"

"The man—that *interesting* man. Where did you find him?"

"He found me."

"Let me guess: on the beach at Keikikai when you were napping. This is exactly what I feared!"

"I told you, he's a tourist."

"You're sure?"

"He's staying in a hotel in Waikiki. It's fine."

"Fine?" Kalei closes his eyes. "You've already marked him."

"There's nothing to worry about."

"You're kahe. You've marked him. He'll find you irresistible."

"It's a dalliance, nothing more. We've both had them before."

"It's different when you're kahe. The risk—"

"—doesn't exist when your lover isn't the descendant of ancient villagers from Lauele." Pua leans her head on Kalei's shoulder. "Think of it this way. He'll scratch my itch and keep me entertained. If I am kahe—and I'm not saying I am—it'll pass. He'll get on a plane back to wherever he came from, and we'll go back to doing what we do best."

"I don't like this, Pua. Not one bit."

"He's a tourist. He'll be gone in a week."

"He could come back."

"I'll make sure he doesn't," she says.

"If they find any part of a body—"

"I don't need a lecture about how the shark hunts will start again. Rabid men slaughtering sharks by the dozens. Panic driving humans to kill indiscriminately. I'm not stupid. No one wants that. If I kill him, I'll leave no trace."

Kalei reaches down and scoops water from the big saltwater pool. It slides like liquid mercury through his fingers as he drizzles it over her feet. She wiggles her toes, flicking the drops away, each one tumbling in the moonlight before landing in the darkness.

Kalei speaks slowly. "Life is good now, Pua. We have a new home in Hohonukai. There's fish in the sea. We can travel wherever we want; humans don't bother us. Life wasn't always this easy."

"Me lying on the beach in the afternoon isn't going to change any of that. Like you said, we can go wherever we want. No one cares."

"What about Aunty Hanalei? She went to this beach and look what happened," Kalei says.

"Aunty Hanalei made the choice to live on land as a human. Her choice, not mine. Not ever," Pua says.

"She fell in love."

"Aunty Hanalei was crazy. Niuhi don't love what they eat," Pua says.

Kalei's lips quirk in a crooked smile. "I used to think that, too, until I met Nanaue's mother."

"But still you left her and your child. We're Niuhi," Pua says. "We belong in the sea."

"Sometimes I wonder how things would be today if I'd chosen to stay with her back then."

Pua laughs. "Too many humans in the world have no room in their imaginations for creatures like us, Kalei. They have no capacity to see the world as it is. Remember the newcomers' horror over Hawaiian wooden gods and sentient stones? A few high chiefs saw how foreigners lived and wanted what they had, so they ordered the villagers to tumble all the old gods to the ground, erasing traditions thousands of years old. Our father Kanaloa saw this coming, I'm convinced of that. Nanaue was only the excuse to hide us away."

"Maybe," he says, "but I miss the old days." He touches her ankle. "Your skin's too dry."

"Thank you for the compliments, brother dear. First my lips are too pale, now my skin looks dry. Do I need to brush my teeth, too?" She bares her teeth at him and pushes his dripping hand away with her foot. "Knock it off."

He shifts beside her on the cold, black lava. "Just trying to help."

"Don't. You're just irritating me."

"Pua?"

"What?"

"You do have to brush your teeth."

"Oh!" She pushes him with her shoulder, happy he's no longer so angry.

He nudges her back. "Well, someone had to tell you."

She thinks for a moment. "You're wrong about

Hohonukai," she says. "It's a place we live; it's not our land."

"We have our land right here at Piko Point," Kalei says.

"Not all of it."

"What's done is done. They won't give us this valley back. Too many humans think they own parts of it now," Kalei says.

Pua says, "I know. It makes me sad."

"Makes me mad." He flicks a hermit crab into the water.

Pua touches his arm. "Kalei, I do know how dangerous it is for me to be here. If I could stop coming, I would."

"You're saying the valley is calling you? Is that it?"

She shrugs. "You ever heard of anyone having an itch like that?"

"Yeah." He grins. "Aunty Hanalei!"

She shoves him. "Shut-up and go if you're just going to make fun of me."

"You're the one talking chicken skin stories." In a high falsetto, he mocks, "Kalei, the land, the 'aina, is calling me; I have to go to the mysterious itching beach or die!"

"Technically, the beach is scratching. I'm itching."

"Whatever, Pua."

They watch the ocean spray dance above the lava as the waves crashed along the breakwater. The rhythm is soothing, like the heartbeat of their mother in the womb. They lean their heads together, lost in thought.

"I have to go away for a while," Kalei says. He lifts

his chin to the ocean. "The ahi are running. Uncle Nalu says he needs my help."

"Do you want me to come?"

He shakes his head. "No. One look at you and Uncle Nalu would know you'd been at the beach."

She touched her face. "I burned?"

"You glow." He flashes his teeth. "But seriously, I want you stay away from this beach." He pauses. "I can't make you."

"No, you can't."

"But will you? Please? For me?"

It's the first time in their lives Kalei has ever asked her for anything. With all her heart, she wants to give it to him, but she can't make a promise she won't keep. She contemplates the stars, waiting for an answer to come.

Kalei sighs and follows her gaze to the sky. "Almost a full moon."

"Yes."

"Father left about an hour ago for the Big Island. When he asks, I'll tell him you went to Molokai for a while."

"To see Kamea. She's due soon. He won't think twice about that."

"At least that will help explain the tan. I hear all she wants to do is lie on the beach. I think she's trying to cook that keiki faster!"

He stands.

"Scratch that beach itch if you must, Pua, but be careful. You cannot afford to be seen, especially around here in the daytime."

He walks along the far edge of the saltwater pool to

where it meets deeper, swifter currents through a passage to the open ocean. He stretches his arms over his head, looking back at her one last time.

"Sunbathing causes cancer, you know. Night is the best beach time."

Moonlight glints off his teeth, stark white against the shadow of his face.

Pua sticks out her tongue. "Since when have you ever worried about cancer? Enjoy your swim, Kalei. Tell Uncle Nalu aloha for me."

His face now grim, he says, "Remember Aunty Hanalei. She went fishing in landlocked waters and never came back."

He twists backward, throwing his body into the darkness. Splashless, he enters the water and dives through the tunnel into the open ocean.

"Show-off," Pua mutters.

She stands, wrapping the sarong tighter. Kalei's right. She needs to eat. She also needs to bathe; her skin feels chapped, rough from the sun, wind, and salt.

A change of clothes would be nice, she thinks. *Perhaps one of the Paris dresses. In five hours the sun will start to rise over the mountains. I hope Justin is an early riser. I can't afford to be in the sun too long.*

6

JUSTIN

Wearing flip-flops and walking across the lava to Piko Point, I wonder if my footwear meets Nili-boy's approval. The dude at Snorkel Bob's just laughed when I asked him if locals ever wear shoes and socks at the beach.

It wasn't a nice laugh.

Whatever.

I rented snorkel gear and paid for a pair of flip-flops, climbed into my car, and headed back to Lauele.

As I carry my gear, I tell myself I'm here to find sharks, but Pua can't find me in *the usual way along the beach* if I'm not here.

I'm not as stupid as I look.

The sun's high in the sky. White pockets of salt and orange cast-off shells of crabs lie scattered across the lava. To my right, five surfers catch waves at Nalupuki. The waves aren't very big, but consistent, and I watch them pump fists and whoop as they ride all the way to shore.

Skirting around tide pools, I see schools of tiny grey fish and striped sergeant majors. The spines of sea urchins poke out from crevasses, and tiny charcoal black snails cling to the rocks.

On the wild ocean side, waves dash against the breakwater. I pause where the water splashes my knees and watch the currents. As long as I stick to the Keikikai side of the lava today, I should be okay. But I came to see sharks, and Nili-boy said they hang out on the Nalupuki side, the side where the surge can smash me into the rocks. To safely get there, I'll have to do a beach entry and swim out with the surfers.

I look toward the beach.

It's a long way back.

Looong way.

Maybe later this afternoon. I've come this far, might as well see it to the end.

I'm almost to Piko Point when I spot a medium-sized yellow dog snoozing on a ratty beach towel next to the biggest tide pool. Nearby is a pair of upside down flip-flops, the center post of the left one patched with a plastic bread tie.

"Hey, girl," I say.

She opens one eye, gives me the once over, and snuggles deeper into the towel.

I'm beneath her contempt.

Challenge accepted.

I set my bag down and walk to the tide pool's edge.

"Keeping an eye on your master's property while he dives, huh? You're a good doggie, aren't you, girl?"

I swear I see her roll her eyes and shake her head before turning her back to me.

"Aw, don't you want to be friends? I'm not going to hurt you."

Did she just chuckle?

Must be the wind.

Looking down into the water, I see different kinds of fish—yellow tangs, purple damsels, and Picasso triggers. A snowflake eel slips back into his home as an octopus hides near coral fans. The water's colder here and the surge is stronger than in the other tide pools— something's different. Stepping to the left, the light hits just right, and I see a large underwater archway leading to open blue water. At my feet are a couple of ledges worn smooth like steps.

Easy in, easy out. Looks like I won't have to do a beach entry after all.

"I bet this is where all the locals come to spearfish and gather lobster. Is your master out there, little girl?"

Not even an ear twitch.

"Hey, Pooch! I'm talking to you."

She squinches her eyes tighter.

I whistle.

Her body tenses, but she doesn't raise her head.

"Sweetie! I'm talking to you."

She tucks her nose to her chest and flattens her ears.

She's trying too hard to ignore me.

I'm going to make her love me.

"C'mon, let's be friends. I have something you'll like. Something my *friends* like."

I walk back to my snorkel bag and take out the snack I bought at Hari's store across the street.

"Beef jerky."

Her tail wraps tighter around her body. I slowly break the seal.

"Teriyaki. Ummmm, smells good."

Her whole body quivers.

I take a piece and wave it around.

"Looks tender."

I put it in my mouth.

"Wow. Delicious."

Her nose wrinkles. She raises her head, narrows her eyes, and chuffs one derisive chuff before flopping completely over to the other side.

I've been dismissed.

"Fine. Be that way. More for me." I tuck the jerky back in my bag, grab my snorkel gear, and sit at the edge of the tide pool. Mask rinsed, snorkel attached, fins on, I ease into the water.

I bob for a bit to get my bearings and then check out the arch. It's a clear shot through it and to the surface on the other side. In the tide pool, I hyperventilate a few times to prepare. One giant breath, and I bend at the waist and jackknife toward the arch.

Glancing back through the shimmery water I see the dog looking down at me, my bag of jerky in her mouth.

She got me.

She got me good.

It only takes four kicks before I'm through the arch.

The world's a little grayer twenty feet below the surface. I feel the surge tug against me, pulling me to deeper water. I relax and let it carry me away from the tunnel, then slowly kick to the surface.

It's ten minutes before the reef settles down enough for the first shark to appear.

I'm taking my time, cruising about fifteen feet above the reef, looking at all the sea life below, when a small white tip reef shark circles around a coral head. It's a juvenile, only about two feet long. I trail it as it glides along the bottom looking for starfish or octopus. I lose it when it turns and heads down through a crack in the reef.

Taking a moment to raise my head and get my bearings, I realize I'm about fifty yards from Piko Point, near where the surfers line up to catch waves.

I fill my lungs and jackknife, heading deep into dark water.

Twenty-five feet down, I wiggle my jaw again to make my ears pop.

Cruising along the bottom, I see them.

Nili-boy wasn't kidding.

Hammerheads, gray reef, blacktip, and even a Galapagos shark all circle below me in an underwater ballet. Most are small, but a couple of the larger ones rest near the bottom where the current rushes over their gills.

I'm in love.

Too soon I have to kick to the surface for air. But I dive again and again, watching how they move and interact, wishing I could stay longer.

Scuba lessons, ASAP, I promise myself. Maybe Snorkel Bob can hook me up.

Another surface, another jackknife, a couple of powerful kicks, and—

Nothing.

This can't be.

Where'd all the fish go?

I surface and dive again, but the reef below is empty

of sharks, butterfly fish, idols, parrot fish—gone, all gone. It's barren reef in all directions.

I'm on my way back up when I get hit from behind by a large brown blur that grabs me and forces me to the surface.

I spit my snorkel out and spin around, trying to figure out what's got my bicep in a vise. Suddenly, another mask surfaces next to me. He lets go of my arm, pulls his snorkel out of his mouth, and says, "We have to get out of the water. NOW!"

"What are you talking about?"

"Can't you feel it?"

"Feel what?" I look for the surfers, but they're headed back to shore.

"Didn't you see?" he says.

"See what? I didn't see anything."

"Exactly," he says. "Even the sharks are hiding. Follow me." He puts his snorkel back in his mouth, holds his fishing spear parallel to the sea bottom, and kicks like an Olympic swimmer back to Piko Point.

When I come through the arch, he's already standing outside the tide pool, rubbing his legs with the ratty towel. He's an older man, part-Hawaiian at least, and he moves with a wiry grace that belies his age. Probably retired and able to spend his days spearfishing.

Lucky.

The yellow dog's nowhere in sight.

I surface and pull off my mask and snorkel.

"Here," he says, holding out his hand, "give 'em to me."

"Thanks."

"'A'ole pilikia," he says, placing my gear next to my bag.

"Ah-oh-lay…?"

He smiles. "'A'ole pilikia. It means no problem, no trouble. Sit on that ledge and take off your fins. Don't worry, no wana—sea urchins—live there."

I swim to the ledge, pull off my fins, and step out of the water.

"Towel?" he asks.

"I've got one, thanks." I dump my fins next to my mask and blot my face with one of the hotel's fluffy white finest, the ones they forbid you to take to the beach.

At their rates, they can afford to loan me a towel.

"You're not from around here," he says.

I slick my hair back and sigh. "Why does everyone keep bringing that up?"

He gestures to my ankle. "You're wearing a ki leaf lei. It threw me off when you didn't know 'a'ole pilikia."

I reach down, tug it off, and stuff it into the pocket of my swim trunks. "It's silly, I know. A kid told me it would protect me from sharks."

"You think it's superstition?"

I tip my head to the right, scrubbing harder with the towel. "Well, come on. If it worked someone would've figured out how to bottle it and make a buck, right?"

The old man opens his mouth, then screws his eyes tight, and snaps his lips closed. He swallows deliberately, then says, "But you wore it anyway."

It's the last thing I expect, a gentle chide that gets under my skin. "You're not wearing one," I say.

He blinks then throws his head back in a great belly laugh. "Oh, I wear one. Mine's just more permanent." He pivots to show me lines of triangles marching down his calves. He holds out his hand. "I'm Kahana."

"Justin." We shake, but then he twists his grip, and suddenly we're clasping thumbs.

"You need to learn how to do this like an island boy," Kahana says, giving my hand one last squeeze.

"I feel like there's a lot of things I need to learn." I point at his spearfishing pole. "That's a Hawaiian sling, right?"

"Yeah." He hands it to me. "Put your hand through the loop. Now twist. Pull back. Now grab the spear right there. See? If you let go, the surgical tubing shoots the spear forward."

"Cool."

"I catch a lot of dinners with this spear. I'm out here most days."

"Nice," I say.

"Beats a nine to five," he says, "even without weekends off."

"Retired?"

He smiles again. "Something like that."

"Hey, what happened out there?" I ask, handing back his spear.

Kahana takes it and throws his towel over his shoulder. "What do you think happened?"

"I'm not sure."

"You didn't feel the ocean telling us something?"

"Get out of the water?"

He nods. "Most of the time we never know why, but

it's important that we listen. We'd outstayed our welcome."

"All the fish went into hiding," I say.

"That's the last sign." He holds out his arm. "The first is the hair on your arms stands up. You get a tingling in your spine. A hot spot forms on the back of your neck. You feel uneasy in the pit of your stomach. That's when you get out of the water. If you wait until you're the last thing swimming in the open, it's probably too late."

I nod. "I'll keep that in mind. Thanks."

Kahana slips his feet into his flip-flops and says, "This isn't a tourist kind of place. What brings you all the way out here?"

"I wanted to see sharks."

"Sharks? Are you crazy?"

"People surf with them daily. You swim with them daily. I wanted to see what they looked like up close."

Kahana rubs the towel across his face. "Pilikia," he says, "with a capital P. Sharks are trouble, brah, and up close they're even more trouble. Don't you have a TV? If you want to see sharks, do it from the safety of your living room. I hear there are entire cable channels devoted to that sort of thing."

"The documentaries only show teeth and fins. I can't see how light and shadows travel across their skin. I need to see how the whole shark moves if I'm going to get it right."

His eyes bug a little when I say this. A thousand words cross his mind, but he discards all except one: "Why?"

It's on the tip of my tongue to say: The truth? Since

yesterday, I can't stop thinking about them. The curves of their spines. The edges of their fins. Their obsidian eyes with lids that snap from the bottom up.

Their rows and rows of teeth.

But I can't say any of that. Instead, I look at Kahana and tell him a secondary truth.

"I'm an art student in search of a project. I have an idea for an art show all about sharks. That's why—"

"—Waikiki Aquarium," he interrupts. "More better you go Waikiki Aquarium. Sit in front of the big and little tanks and sketch to your heart's delight. There you can get up close and personal with sharks without having to chase them over a reef. If you're feeling super adventurous, head to Sea Life Park. Costs more, though." He pauses to see if I'm hearing what he's trying to say. His teeth worry his lower lip. "You saw the sign at the pavilion, right?"

"Yeah."

"It's not a joke. There's no reason for you to reck-lessly endanger yourself here."

Mentally, I take a step back. *Recklessly endanger? I'm a grown man, not a five-year-old.*

I say, "But it's okay for you to recklessly endanger yourself, right? It's what you do, every day you're out here hunting for dinner." I wince at my whiny tone. I don't mean it, but I can't help it.

His arm sweeps the ocean all the way to the beach. "This is my home. I don't have a choice. You do." He waits a beat, then adds, "You don't want to bite off more than you can chew, Justin. Things are not normal out there right now. I don't know why. I also don't want you—or anybody else—getting hurt."

I open my mouth to say something, anything, but before I do, there's a yip right behind me. I jump.

"Ah, 'Ilima," says Kahana, "there you are."

I spin around to see the jerky thief. "Finally came back for your master, huh?" I say.

"Master?" Kahana says. "Is that what you think?" He chuckles and wipes his eyes. "Oh, man. You hear that, 'Ilima? Master! That means I'm the boss!"

'Ilima chuffs once and pants, tongue lolling past her chin.

Is that a smile?

"Ah, well," says Kahana. "No fish today. Looks like we're having Spam and rice for dinner, 'Ilima." Kahana hefts his spear and gives me a tip of his chin. "Laters, brah. Like I said, better you go Waikiki Aquarium. It's dangerous here. But if you do come back, wear that ki leaf lei. It doesn't matter what you believe, Justin, only what the sharks do. Come, 'Ilima. We go."

He takes only a couple of steps toward shore before something on the lava catches his eye. Picking it up, he reaches back and hands me the empty jerky bag. "Yours, yeah? Make sure it gets in a rubbish can. Nobody likes swimming in a landfill."

"Right," I say, taking the wrapper.

Scolded like I'm five again.

I swear the dog is laughing at me.

I scowl at her, and she gives her whole body a shake that ends in an innocent *who, me?* look.

There's something up with that dog.

"I'll make sure the trash gets where it belongs. Thanks for everything."

"No problem," he says.

I tuck the wrapper into my pocket next to the soggy ki leaf lei and watch as Kahana makes his way to the pavilion, 'Ilima leading the way.

"Yeah," I mutter. "No problem. Ah-oh-lay-some-thing-easy-for-you-to-say."

7

JUSTIN

At the showers, I rinse off my gear before stepping into the cold spray to scrub the salt out of my hair and the sand off my feet. My mind swims with images of sharks. How do I recreate the feeling—

Paint the floor.

It bursts into my brain like a symphony.

Put the audience in a bubble floating in the sea. A circular wall mural of ocean life from a center perspective that shatters as they walk. Paint the floor to look like bottom of the ocean as seen through glass, the ceiling like looking up through water to sunlight. Suspend sculptures throughout the exhibit space. Diffuse the light and layer shadows. Use fans to create currents against the skin and to move schools of fish strung on mobiles. Use humidifiers to waft salt scents through the air. Add an airlock to the room to increase the feeling of pressure in ears and sinuses. Play the sounds of fish nibbling, shellfish snapping, the roar of surf as it rolls against the shore, the distant calls of whales...

I'm so excited, hair raises along my arms.

Finally, a vision for my dissertation. *I'll bring the ocean to the landlocked in the form of a bubble under the sea. An art show like this could do more than entertain, it could educate, engage, and inspire. School kids could —*

"Aloha, Justin."

I wipe water out of my eyes and smile. "You found me."

Pua laughs. "Was there any doubt?"

I turn off the water and grab my towel. In a deceptively simple green and yellow sundress, she's stunning.

"That you could find me? No," I say. "That you'd want to, well, yeah."

She shifts her weight. "Why wouldn't I?"

"Are you kidding? Look at you in that Givenchy dress, oozing elegance. Look at me all covered in sand. You're so out of my league."

She walks over and places her hand on my arm. "I don't think so," she says.

It's like I've been hit by lightning. Every nerve in my body lights up. A blush warms from the back of my neck to my toes. I feel like a seventh grader at my first dance.

New Me hisses, "Get a grip. If she figures out how completely uncool you are, it's over."

I try for nonchalant. "You're too kind."

At least this time my voice doesn't break.

She squeezes my arm and says, "I find you interesting, Justin. I'd like to get to know you better."

I swallow and say, "What do you have in mind?"

She leans close and purrs, "Do you like games?"

Games?

I think of the way she inhaled me on the beach.

"Like—" I clear my throat, "like video games?"

The corner of her mouth pulls slyly. "No," she says. "What I have in mind is nothing like video games."

Oh, Lord. Am I going to need a safe word?

She turns and with a single come-hither glance over her shoulder, walks out of sight around the pavilion. I grab my stuff and scramble to follow. When I round the corner, she's not there.

I knew it.

Punked.

"Pua?"

"In here," she calls. "The other side of the oleander hedge."

It takes me a moment, but then I spot the opening. It's narrow, almost too narrow, and I push my way through, dragging my snorkel gear behind me.

It's a scene from another century.

The area is intimate, surrounded by ten-foot oleander bushes on three sides, but open to an ocean view overlooking the entire bay. Shading the space are two towering trees bursting with fragrant white and yellow flowers. The grass beneath them is stunted and scruffy, but it's mostly covered by a large woven mat. On the mat are a couple of lounging pillows, a bowl of fresh fruit, a tall gourd with coconut shell cups, and a small wooden board dotted with black and white pebbles.

"This is amazing."

Pua slips a flower behind her right ear, sinks onto the mat, and reclines against a pillow.

"Want to play?" she asks.

It's every male teenage fantasy come true.

I freeze.

In my head, Sasha laughs. "You are swimming soooo over your head!"

Shut up, Sasha!

"Um…"

"Sit," Pua says and pats the mat beside her.

"I'm wet," I blurt.

She raises an eyebrow.

"I mean, my swim trunks. From the shower."

"It's fine. This lauhala mat has seen worse," she says. "Unless you'd be more comfortable with them off?"

"No!" I squeak.

Her eyes light up.

I hastily clear my throat again. "I mean, no, thanks. I'm good. I'm sure they'll dry faster on. Unless, you know, you want me to. Do you want me to? No! Don't answer. I'm just going to—"

I walk over to the mat, slip off my flip-flops, and sit crisscross apple sauce, hands clasped in my lap.

In a corner of my mind, Sasha plops down in an easy chair with a monster bucket of popcorn. "This is going to be good."

I clench my jaw and try to ignore her.

"Comfy?" Pua asks.

"Uh-huh," I mumble.

"You don't look comfortable."

Sasha crams a handful of popcorn in her mouth.

"I'm fine," I say.

From an imaginary side table, Sasha grabs a drink

and starts sucking on the straw. When she sees me watching her, she gives me an enthusiastic thumbs up.

Bitch.

Pua gestures to the board. "Konane. Ever played?"

"No."

"It's not complicated. Black lava versus white coral pieces, alternating stones. This board is an eight by eight grid." She reaches out and removes a black lava rock and a white piece of coral from the center of the board. "Black goes first. You move by jumping over your opponent's stone into an empty space. The eaten stone is removed. You can only move in a straight line —no turns or diagonals. Jump as many of your opponent's stones as you choose as long as each jump lands in an open space and continues in a straight line. The winner is the one who can still make a move."

Is she joking?

Is making a move some kind of island code?

I look from the board to her face. She's smiling, but there's a definite air of challenge about her.

"Unless you don't think you can beat me," she says.

Game on!

I reach out and pick up a black stone, deftly jump over a white piece, and remove it from the board. Quick as a cat, she jumps and removes one of my pieces. The game progresses quickly, clearing out the center until I'm forced to start moving my edge pieces.

Finally, I have to stop and study the board. "This is harder than it looks," I say.

"It's not just a children's game. Everyone played konane. Chiefs and commoners competed in high stakes tournaments. Kamehameha the Great was said to be unbeatable."

"But you don't believe that."

"Everyone loses some time," she says.

"But he was the Great!" I say.

"Yes, he was very, very good."

"But you're better."

"Of course." A triple jump clears most of my remaining pieces. "I win," she says.

I blink.

"You ambushed me!"

She laughs. "Not bad for your first game."

"Again!"

"I warn you; I won't take it easy on you."

"It's not your nature," I say.

She smiles that inscrutable smile and starts to reset the board. "No," she says quietly, "it's not."

After the losing the second and then a third game, Pua pushes a pillow toward me. "Lie down. Get comfortable."

I prop myself on my side and help her reset the board.

"Something to drink?" she asks.

"Sure."

She pours pink liquid into a coconut cup and hands it to me. "Guava juice with a little liliko'i mixed in."

"What's that?"

"Passion fruit. Shall I make the first move or do you want to?"

Once again, I freeze.

Sasha perks up. "Finally," she mutters. "This whole

thing's dragging on longer than ketchup out of a bottle."

Nope. Buh-bye, Sasha! Hope all that buttered popcorn goes right to your thighs.

I mentally slam the door in Sasha's outraged face.

Feels so good, I slam it twice.

"Justin?" says Pua.

I blink and snap back to the present. "I'll follow your lead, Pua, whatever you want to do."

She reaches out and removes two markers.

I have to admit, I'm a little disappointed.

We begin again.

"What were you thinking about back at the showers?" Pua asks. "You had such a look of wonder on your face." Her black jumps my white.

It's early in the game, so strategy doesn't matter much. All the big decisions happen in the end. I quickly jump the black piece closest to me and remove it from the board.

I say, "I was thinking about an art project to complete my master's degree. What if people could experience what it was like to be underwater without getting wet?"

"The word you're looking for is submarine," says Pua. "Or Jacque Cousteau."

"What?"

"The French—oh, never mind," she says with a double-jump.

My white coral eats another lava stone. "The world is more than seventy-percent ocean, and most people have never experienced what it's like to swim with fish," I counter.

Pua rolls her eyes. "They aren't missing much."

"I don't believe you. You're just jaded from living in paradise." I motion to Piko Point. "The sharks out there—"

In the act of removing a piece from the board, Pua stills. She waits until I meet her eyes. "What do you know about the sharks out there?" she spits.

Where's this white-hot anger coming from?

No. I'm reading this wrong. She's just concerned for me. That's all.

"Just what I observed snorkeling with them this morning. The sharks are why I came back to Lauele. Well, one of the reasons," I tease.

She pulls away from the game and starts rearranging the fruit in the bowl.

Oh, crap. I've somehow screwed the pooch.

"Who told you about the sharks off Piko Point?" she bites, every line in her body tighter than a drawn bow.

I open my mouth to say Nili-boy, but realize I can't tell her that. She's far too upset about something and Lauele's too small for them not to know each other. She'll eat him alive for spilling the beans about sharks. How—

Oh, yeah.

The stupid sign.

"I saw the sign."

"What sign?"

"The one warning people about sharks at the pavilion. People wouldn't post that without a reason, right?" I remove another stone. "Your turn."

She reaches out and moves stones without looking at the board.

This has gone way south.

In my head, Sasha's beating on the door, wanting to get out. I put a double-lock on it and take a deep breath.

"I'm sorry I scared you by ignoring the sign and snorkeling off Piko Point. I know how terrifying sharks can be to people—"

Was that a cough or a laugh?

I press on.

"—but not all sharks are dangerous. They aren't mindless eating machines hell-bent on eating people. *Jaws* gave them all a bad rap."

Pua won't look at me. She turns further away.

I say, "I think if more people knew that, they'd care more about sharks. They'd want to protect them."

Is she biting her lip?

Her shoulders are shaking.

Oh, no.

Is she crying?

"Pua, it's okay. I won't go back out there—not until you feel okay about it. In the meantime, we can do some observations and sketches together at the Waikiki Aquarium—"

She spins toward me, hissing like a wildcat. "The Aquarium? THE AQUARIUM? You want to take me to that soul-less morgue of death, disease, and confinement?"

"Uh—"

"How dare you? How dare you support the enslavement of free creatures? You're just like all the rest!"

Holy crap! How did we get here?

"Wait a minute! I never thought about aquariums like that. But doesn't that mean what I'm trying to do is a good thing? My art show will do all that an aquarium does to bring the ocean to people without harming a single sea creature. People go to aquariums because they can't dive or don't live by the beach. Aquariums show them an undersea world full of wonder. It's like dolphins—"

She throws her hands wide. "Dolphins? Dolphins? Of course people like dolphins. You know why they're smiling all the time? Because they're the stupidest suck-ups in the sea."

Wow.

She just doesn't get it.

"Pua, people just don't like dolphins; they adore dolphins. And what people love, they protect," I say.

She's breathing hard, but she's listening.

I think.

"Pua, when was the last time you played in the ocean? Splashed in the waves?"

She narrows her eyes and sets her jaw. "I don't *play* in the ocean."

"See, that's what I'm talking about. When did you last see a sunset from a boat deck?"

"I—"

"Never, I know. That's something tourists do, not locals. You're like someone who lives in the alps and never skis. I'm going to change that—"

"No."

"What?"

"You're not going to change me, Justin. I am exactly what I am. Nothing more, nothing less."

"Whoa, you're taking this all wrong." I look down at

the board, frustrated. "You said konane was a high stakes game. Let's raise the stakes."

"Brave words from someone who's never won a game."

"I have two tickets for a catamaran snorkeling adventure tomorrow. If I win, you have to come with me and play tourist."

"And if I win?"

"Name it," I say.

"Later," she says.

Later? What does that mean?

"Bets need to be two ways, Pua. What would make you as happy as I will be if you go snorkeling with me tomorrow? Dinner at a fancy restaurant? New shoes? Tickets to a concert? Me to shave my head?"

Shave my head? What am I saying?

She looks down her nose at me. "I don't know what will make me happy, yet. If you want to bet, you'll have to agree to whatever I choose when I choose it."

How bad could it be?

"Okay," I say. "You can decide later. But I have veto power over head-shaving or piercings or tattoos. Deal?"

"Deal," Pua says. "Your move."

We turn our attention back to the board.

In one glance I see exactly what I need to do to win. Her pieces are in perfect position for mine to double and triple jump. All I have to do is remove more of her pieces than she can of mine, and I'll win.

I make my first triple jump move and take three of her stones from the board.

She reaches out and eats one of my pieces. "That's game," she says.

"Impossible. I have way more pieces than you!"

"That's still game. Konane is not about having the most pieces, it's about having an option to move. You don't. You lose."

I sit up and study the board. *She's right.*

"You won, Pua. Good game. Guess you don't have to go snorkeling with me tomorrow."

"My father thinks like you," she says out of the blue. "He allows aquariums because he believes they help humans understand that they are only one piece in an interconnected world."

"Allows?" I tip my head back and finish my drink. "Is your father in government or something?"

"Or something."

She gathers the stones and puts them in a pouch.

Slowly, she nods. "The aquarium *is* the right place for you to sketch, Justin, better than off Piko Point. Your idea of an art show that brings the ocean to land is worth pursuing."

"Thanks."

I think?

She stands and smooths the front of her dress.

I jump to my feet, too.

She says, "I'll go on the catamaran tomorrow—"

"That's—"

She holds up her hand. "Not because of the game, but because you asked me to."

I can't stop grinning.

"I'll pick you up. Where—"

"I'll meet you there," she says, and before I can say anything else, she slips through the oleander bushes.

"Wait! You don't know the time or the place or anything!" I call.

Her laughter carries through the hedge. "Don't worry. I'll find you."

"Kewalo Basin! 3:30 pm! The *Ariel*!" I shout.

But she's gone.

8

PUA

Pua leaps into the ocean at Piko Point, changing
from human to shark the moment the water
touches her skin. Coolness washes over her
gills as she flicks her tail once to propel herself through
the arch and into the wild blue.

As the water churns, bubbles rise.

She turns and snap, snap, snaps at the silly, frivolous
things, her jaws unhinged and gulp, gulp, gulping.

Humans are messy, she thinks. *So emotional. So sincere.
So much easier to be a shark.*

She doesn't have to scan the reef to know that it's
empty. Sea creatures know their places. They don't
lecture her—her!—about sharks or the benefits of
aquariums. They don't try to tell her how wonderful
dolphins are.

Dolphins taste like chicken, she smirks. *Warm-blooded
and juicy.*

His arrogance is staggering.

He thinks he can persuade humans to love sharks with

pretty pictures and toys. It's all about them, of course. He's given no thought to what sharks want or need.

They definitely don't need humans.

The world would be such a better place without them and their noisy, polluting ways.

She arches her back and rolls in the water.

Damn, that itch beneath my dorsal fin!

Father, I don't know why you're punishing me like this. As the Great Ocean God Kanaloa, on pain of death to me, my lover, and son, you forbade me from becoming a mother, something even the lowest invertebrate in your kingdom is allowed to do. But you've also given me an itch that's driving me insane, and the only cure is to break your kapu. Why won't you take this urge away from me and let me return to creature I used to be?

It's not fair, Father.

You made me who I am. You know my nature.

The consequences are yours.

9

JUSTIN

S he's late.

I'm standing at the end of the gangway, looking back to the entrance to the docks at Kewalo Basin Harbor. All the passengers but me are already aboard the *Ariel*, sipping drinks and shooting the breeze. The captain leans over the railing.

"We gotta go, man," he says.

"Just a few minutes more," I plead.

"We're already fifteen minutes past our departure time. People want to see the turtles."

"Give them another round of drinks on me."

"Can't dude. You coming or not?"

"I—"

He softens. "I get it. It happens a lot. People meet on vacation. There's an instant connection. You're certain you've met your soulmate. But then things look different in the morning. Chin up. There's always more fish in the sea."

"Not like this one," I say.

"Why don't you come aboard? You've already paid for the trip. Who knows, we might get lucky and see some dolphins. Everybody loves dolphins."

She's not coming.

I'm never going to see her again.

Sasha looks up from her newspaper and coffee. "Told you," she says and turns a page.

For the last time, you're not real. Get out of my head.

She blows me a kiss that turns into a raspberry. "I'm as real as you're going to get, sugar. Get used to it."

"Hey!" says the captain. "Tick-tock."

I walk up the gangway as the deckhands cast off.

"Finally," I hear an overweight man say to his sunburned wife.

"Shhhh!" she says. "Don't be rude!" She thrusts out her hand as I squeeze past. "I'm Kari with an i from Oklahoma. This is Earl."

"Hi Kari. I'm Justin."

"Oh, my hell," says Earl. "I need another drink."

"Earl!" says Kari. "We just had lunch."

"It's five o'clock somewhere."

Earl gets up and heads to the bar.

"Don't mind him. He's just a little nervous to be snorkeling." She looks around and mouths *sharks*.

"Sharks aren't anything to be afraid of," I say.

"I read on the internet that they eat turtles. Aren't we going to be swimming with turtles?" says a bomb-shell in a blue bikini.

Her boyfriend flexes his bicep as he puts his arm around her. "Relax, Babe. I got you."

A teenage goth chick rolls her eyes and snaps her

gum. "If a shark wants you, there's nothing you can do."

"Hey," interrupts a deckhand with a smile and a tray of drinks. "No shark talk. Captain's rules. Orange juice?"

"No, thanks," I say.

"Sunscreen?" Kari waves a Costco-sized bottle at me. "Gotta protect your nose, you know." *Skin cancer,* she mouths.

I feel the urge to join Earl in something stronger.

"Excuse me," I say and head to the galley.

It takes us about half an hour to get to the snorkel site. Three other tour boats are already anchored. The dive master starts his safety spiel about staying near the boat and remembering we're on the *Ariel* and not the *Kahalakai.* As he demonstrates the proper way to inflate a snorkel vest, he says nothing about sharks or about what not to touch. Looking down into the water, I figure the reef's twenty feet below us. Wearing a snorkel vest, it's going to be tough to get that deep. Under protest, Goth Girl finally puts a vest on, but stubbornly refuses to inflate it.

"Sweetie, what if you drown?" her mother wails.

"Then it won't matter. I'll be dead."

I hoist my bottle of beer to her.

I like her.

Once all the fins are sorted and masks dotted with goo, the passengers start flopping into the water. Bombshell squeals when Biceps lifts her over the side and drops her in.

What a douche.

I bet they're perfect together.

"Getting in?" I say to Earl.

"Ppfft," he says.

I take that as a no.

Once it's just me and Earl and the deckhands, the captain swings by. "Not getting in?"

I shrug. "Seems rather pointless. You can't see anything that doesn't come up to you when you're wearing a vest. Too hard to kick down. Got any little boxes of cornflakes or cans of Cheez Whiz?"

He laughs. "The Great State of Hawaii frowns on that kind of behavior. Not good for the fish or reef."

"Great for the tourists, though."

"I tell you what. You wanna jump in without a vest, be my guest."

"Your dive master was pretty strict about that."

"That girl was under eighteen with nervous parents. You're an adult who knows about baiting fish with cornflakes and Cheez Whiz. I'll chance it."

I hand my empty bottle to the bartender. "Set my buddy Earl up with another," I say and slip him a twenty.

I put my mask and snorkel on and don't bother with the ladder.

The cold water shocks what little buzz I had going right out of my head.

What am I doing?

I should just cut my losses and head back to Cali.

I blow water out of my snorkel, put my head down, and kick away from the crowds and the boats.

The water's crystal clear, so I stop kicking and just float facedown for a while. The sunlight makes zebra stripes out of the shadows of the ripples. There're some barrel sponges and patches of something purplish on the reef, but most of the fish stay well away from me.

Is that an octopus?

Better check where the boat's at.

Don't want to get too far.

As I raise my head and turn, the shadow of something big, really big, passes below me. I whip around, but I don't see it. I tread water in a circle, my head on a swivel.

"Hey," somebody calls. "Where'd all the fish go?"

Something flashes past the corner of my eye. I spin, but I'm too slow.

The boat's 50 yards away.

My heart's pounding.

Don't be ridiculous.

You're psyching yourself out.

"Dah-dum," says Sasha. "Dah-dum."

Another shadow, this one circling to the left.

"Dah-dum. Dahdumdahdumdahdum—"

Knock it off, Sasha!

It's all in my head.

FLASH.

No! I definitely saw something that time.

I fill my lungs and prepare to break the world record for a 50 yard snorkel dash. I lean forward, spread my legs for a scissor kick—

BAM!

Something reaches around my neck and squeezes.

"Miss me?" she says.

"Aiiiiiii," I scream and promptly swallow water.

Pua wraps her arms around my chest and hauls me to the surface. "It's okay," she says. "You're with me."

"Pua! Where? How?" I sputter.

"Told you I'd find you."

She's bobbing upright, barely treading water to stay at the surface. She's wearing a white bikini that shows off her golden tan.

And a whole lot more.

"Where's your snorkel gear?"

"Snorkel gear is for wimps," she says.

"Where's your boat?"

"Over there," she points.

Two of the other boats are underway, heading in different directions, while the third one's pulling anchor.

"Pua! Your boat left!"

She shrugs.

I look to my boat. The dive master's waving us all back to the catamaran. "Come back," he calls. "We're going to a better spot. All the turtles have left."

I shake my head. "Your boat must have miscounted its passengers! Let's get to my boat and tell the captain. C'mon."

We make our way to the *Ariel* and wait for the others to board. When it's just us left, Pua motions me ahead. I kick to the stairs, hand my mask, snorkel, and fins to the deck hand, and climb up. The deckhand leans past me to give Pua a hand.

I see his face go white.

I barely have time to break his fall before his head hits the deck when he faints.

There's commotion and confusion as people rush to us.

"Is he okay?"

"What happened?"

"Bring him here. Somebody get the first aid kit."

"Should we call the Coast Guard?"

"I've got a pulse. He's breathing. Let's just give him some space."

In the eye of the hurricane, I look up and see Pua standing on the deck, watching us. The captain spots her when he comes running from the galley with the first aid kit. He stops cold.

"She's with me," I say.

They regard each other for one long moment. The captain dips his head. Pua smiles and leans against the railing. Time speeds up. The captain kneels next to me.

"Keanu," he says to the deckhand.

"I think he fainted," I say.

"Keanu." The captain pats the deckhand's cheek. "C'mon, man. It's going to be all right."

Keanu jerks awake. "Knee-oooo-he," he moans.

The captain puts his hand over Keanu's mouth. "Shhhhhh," he whispers. "I know. Be cool."

Kari with an i holds out a baggie full of ice. "For his knee," she says.

"What?" says the captain.

"Didn't he just say he hurt it?"

"Oh. Yeah. Thanks," says the captain. Together we help Keanu sit up.

"For your sore *knee*," says the captain.

Still dazed, Keanu clasps the bag first to his left knee, then to his right.

Man, he hit his head harder than I thought.

The captain stands and addresses the crowd.

"He's fine, folks. But I just got word that conditions

aren't good for snorkeling. There's a storm blowing in, so we're going to have to head back to the harbor now."

"What? No turtles, late start, early return, what a rip-off!"

The captain says, "I know it's a bummer, but safety is our number one priority. But our number two priority is a good time. Drinks are on the house until we get to the harbor."

The crowd cheers.

The captain continues. "After you get your whistle wet, see Becky—wave your hand, Becky—see Becky before you exit the boat. She'll either refund your money or give you a ticket for another day—your choice."

"That's more like it!"

"Becky, turn up the music. Maybe we can tempt some dolphins to put on a show for us."

"Yeah!"

The music starts to boom. People drift away, some to the bar, others to the sun decks.

"Let's go to the bow," Pua says, taking my hand and pulling. At our feet, Keanu closes his eyes and moans. She doesn't even spare him a glance. "Don't worry. He's fine."

"Just a second," I tell her.

I reach out and touch the captain's shoulder. "Hey, Captain, I need to report something."

He turns, wary. His eyes shoot past me to Pua. "I already know," he says.

"Somebody already radioed you about a missing passenger? I bet the other captain was having kittens once he realized he'd left someone behind."

"Um—"

"My friend Pua is the one they left behind. It's unconscionable. Imagine if we hadn't been here to pick her up."

Pua puts her chin on my shoulder and leans over. "Yes, Captain. Just. Imagine."

The captain swallows. "We're, um, honored to be of service."

"C'mon, Justin," she says, "let's head to the front. I bet we'll see dolphins. Lots of dolphins. People like a show, don't they, Captain?"

He nods.

"Don't worry," Pua says as she breezes past, "I'm only here for Justin. He thinks I need to gain a deeper appreciation for the sea."

The Captain squeezes his eyes tight. "Tourists," he says. "Heaven helps us."

"Oooo!" Pua squeals. "Look!"

All around the boat, the water begins to roil. Suddenly, a dolphin leaps out of the water, his entire body as high as the safety railing. More appear, surfing the wake off the bow. Pacing us on either side are a dozen, then two dozen, then too many to count.

"It's a giant pod of dolphins," Kari says. "One huge family!"

"Whoa," says Biceps.

"Quick! Let's get a dolphin selfie," says Bombshell.

When the cell phones come out, the dolphins go nuts: spinning, leaping, clicking and squeaking. There's so much spray from their blowholes that it drifts over the water like smoke.

"Earl! Earl!" shouts Kari, "Come see the babies!"

Earl shakes his head and buries his nose in a beer.

"You're missing it!"

People line every vantage spot along the boat. Goth Girl puts her black lipstick in her pocket as she stands next to me, a frown on her face. "This is weird," she says.

"I think it's amazing," I say.

"But there are three kinds of dolphins out there." She points. "Those are spinners, those are spotted, and those bigger ones off the bow are bottlenose." Pua locks like a laser onto Goth Girl. "It's like a school assembly where the principal makes the jocks, nerds, and drama kids dance together."

Pua narrows her eyes. "You're saying it's a little too much?"

Becky interrupts with a tray of plastic champagne flutes. "Compliments of the captain."

I take two and hand one to Pua. When Goth Girl reaches for one, Becky tilts the tray away. "Sorry, adults only. I'll bring you a soda in a minute." Over Becky's shoulder a dolphin tail walks.

Biceps pushes between us. "Babe! You gotta see this."

A mama dolphin paces the ship as her baby circles and jumps.

Bombshell squeezes in. "It's so cute I want to die!" She grabs his shoulder. "I want one! They're so little, I bet they'd fit in our pond."

Goth Girl says, "A freshwater pond?"

Bombshell says, "Yes! Behind our apartment. Oh, it would be perfect!"

"Dolphins need saltwater—"

"No, they don't! They breathe air, not water like fish," says Bombshell. "They can live anywhere there's air. Ain't that right, Babe?"

"You know it, Babe. I bet Joey could catch us one the next time he's in the Gulf."

"You'd take a baby from its mother?" Pua asks.

"Oh, honey, it's not like that," Bombshell says. "They're fish. It don't mean the same to them."

Goth Girl says, "Dolphins are mammals, not fish."

Bombshell waves her hand. "Whatever. You know what I mean."

Pua stares for a moment at her champagne. Off the bow, dolphins are doing front flips.

"Are you okay?" I ask. "Do you want to get out of the sun?"

"I need some space." As Pua turns away from the rail, the dolphins suddenly submerge and disappear.

"Aww," Kari says. "Where'd they go?"

"Here," Pua says, handing Goth Girl her champagne.

"Thanks!"

"Don't you want it?" I ask.

Pua gives me her Mona Lisa smile. "I've had more than enough of bubbles lately."

"Want me to get you some water?"

"No. Let's head to the least crowded part of the boat," she says.

As we climb the ladder to the top deck, people spot three distinct groups of dolphins heading away from our boat.

"Looks like she was right," I say. "Three different

kinds of dolphins, not one big family pod. Wonder why."

Pua brushes the hair out of her face. "Dolphins, whales, sharks—who can tell them apart?"

"See, that's why I think—"

The captain comes over the loudspeaker. "Folks, we'll be at the dock in five minutes. Time to finish your drinks, gather all your belongings, and get ready to disembark. If you haven't gotten your vouchers, be sure to see Becky. On behalf of the crew of the *Ariel*, we hope your island vacation continues to be everything you imagined. Aloha!"

We're the last ones off the boat.

At the gangway the captain hands Pua a sarong. "With your stuff lost on another catamaran, I thought you might like this," he says. "A tourist left it behind last week."

Pua smiles and wraps the orange and green tie-dye sarong into a dress. "Castoffs are my favorite kind," she says. "Smooth sailing, Captain."

"With your blessing, it's sure to be." He bows a little as she passes down the gangway. I move to follow, but he grabs my arm and pulls me close. "Be careful," he whispers. "She's—"

"Not your typical island girl? Told you," I say.

He takes a breath to say more, but then shakes his head and releases my arm.

"Good luck to you, Justin," he says. "I'll be praying it goes well for you."

I wink. "You and me both!"

JUSTIN

"**I**'m parked over here. Where's your car?" I ask.

"I don't have one," Pua says.

I grin. "You were that sure you'd find me?"

"It's not hard. You're very predictable."

I unlock the doors and throw my snorkel gear in the back. "Okay, Smarty-pants, what do I want to do now?" I wiggle my eyebrows suggestively.

"Not that," she says. "Food now." She slides into the passenger seat. "That's later."

In my own private corner of imaginary hell, Sasha stands with her mouth open.

Suck it, Sasha.

I say, "I have a reservation for us at L'Couteux—"

"No."

I blink. "It's rated—"

"No."

"Where then? Pua, I want to take you somewhere nice. You mean a lot to me—"

"Start the car. Let's head to Lauele. I know just the place."

I hop in and turn the ignition. Lava-hot air explodes from the vents. "Sorry, sorry!" I say, frantically rolling the windows down. "There's no air conditioning!"

Pua gathers her hair, twists, and magically creates a bun on the top of her head. "What are you talking about? That's what windows are for." She reaches over and steals my sunglasses from the console. "That's better. The sun is always so bright." She leans back in her seat, sighs, and closes her eyes. "It's toasty warm in here, nothing like the deep ocean. To experience anything like this, you have to get close to a volcano."

"Watching a volcano erupt underwater would be incredible."

"Not really," she says. "Nobody wants to swim in sulfur. Itchy."

"I'd scratch your itch."

"Later," she says with another huge sigh.

All her bones melt.

Is she going to sleep?

Sasha rears her head. "Dude, she is totally going to sleep. It's a long drive in a sweltering car. She didn't want to go to dinner at the best restaurant in Honolulu. She wants you to take her back to Lauele so she can get away from your sorry ass. Read between the lines."

She had fun on the boat.

"Which part? The part where she didn't meet you at the dock, the part where she got left behind, or the part where her stuff got lost, so she's wearing a reject from the lost and found?"

The dolphins were cool. Everybody loved the dolphins.

"You sure about that?" Sasha gets comfy on pool lounger, sipping an umbrella drink.

"Pua?" I say.

"Hmmm?"

"What did you think of the dolphins?"

"The dolphins?"

"Yeah. I know we didn't get a chance to snorkel along the reef much, but did you see how excited people got seeing dolphins in the wild? It's why I want to create my art exhibit."

"You want to make people feel like they can steal a baby dolphin from the ocean and put it in their fresh-water pond?"

"Those two don't count. They're idiots."

"Most people are."

"But that's why we need to educate them."

"It's a waste of time. Humans believe they are the most important creatures on the planet. Everything and everyone belongs to them. It's their nature to destroy. You can't go against nature. Might was well yell at the waves to stay away from the shore."

I turn onto the highway and head out of the city, thinking about what she's saying. "You sound angry."

She rolls her head on her shoulders. "Not angry. There's no sense in getting angry when a toddler does what toddlers do."

"That's harsh. What about Goth Girl—the one with the black lipstick. Do you think she's like the two who wanted a baby dolphin?"

Pua purses her lips. "No. She's aware. If more were

like her, I'd have hope, but she's the exception that proves the rule."

"You don't believe in the power of one? One voice, one person, can change the world."

"Humans are herd animals."

I laugh. "But even herds have leaders."

"If you say so."

At highway speeds, the wind is whipping through the car. Tendrils of hair, loose from her bun, flail like octopus tentacles around her face.

"You didn't like the boat," I say.

"I liked it fine," she says. "Just don't fool yourself into thinking these kinds of ocean encounters are more than superficial entertainment. It's a holiday, a break in routine, for everybody."

She shakes her hair loose, and the sweet smell of sandalwood and something I can't put my finger on—salt, maybe?—fills the car. Her hair brushes against my lips. She leans her head toward her lap and sweeps her hair up, twisting tighter and tighter until another knot forms on the top of her head.

"Hair," she grumbles. "I never know what to do with it."

"Please promise me you'll never cut it," I say.

"Cut it?"

"Yeah. No bobs or bangs or layers. It's beautiful just the way it is."

"Cut it?" She wrinkles her nose. "You can do that?"

The light through the windshield kisses her cheeks, her chin, and the long graceful line of her neck that ends in the hollow at the base of her throat.

I want to bury my nose in it and blaze a trail of kisses to her belly button.

I'm in love.

From her imaginary lounge chair, Sasha pulls out a fan.

"No, Justin," Sasha says. "You're in heat."

11

PUA

It's hot.

Pua feels it all the way to the pit of her stomach. She doesn't have to glance at Justin to see that he's feeling it, too.

The air on her skin is almost too much. Soon she won't be able to stand the clothes she's wearing.

Her scent is changing. Even Justin's puny nose can tell. Behind the sunglasses, she watches as his nostril flare; his eyes dilate and darken with desire.

She runs her finger over the skin between her knee and the edge of the sarong, over and over, in little circles, and shudders.

Can I do this again?

She remembers other lovers, some tender, some fierce, and wonders what Justin will be like.

She inhales and uses her tongue to parse the scents flowing through the back of her throat.

Man sweat.

Soap.

Salt.

A mishmash of the people from the boat.

And something—just a hint—

The ghost of someone special, a woman, but not for a while.

There's a bitter afternote of heartbreak there.

Grateful. He'll be a grateful lover.

And I will finally put that itch to rest.

At least this time, I won't have to kill him.

It's the one thing tourists are good for.

12

JUSTIN

When we round the last curve that leads to the Lauele, I turn to Pua. "Where's the restaurant?"

"Just pull into the parking lot at the pavilion," she says.

"You don't want to eat?"

"I need to eat. You do, too, to keep your strength up. You're no good to me weak."

Weak? Right now I can pound nails.

"Then where—"

"Just park."

I pull into a stall and shut off the engine. The sky is purple, rose, and gold as the sun sinks into the ocean.

Pua opens her door and steps out. When I start to follow, she leans back down. "Why don't you wait by the tables and watch the sunset? I'll bring us something from Hari's."

"I'll go with you."

"No. I need a minute to freshen up. I'll just pop into

Hari's and be right back." She shuts the door and starts across the parking lot.

I scramble out of the car. "Wait! You don't have your purse!"

She waves without looking back.

"How are you going to pay without any money?"

She calls over her shoulder, "You worry about the strangest things."

I watch as she sashays across the street and disappears into the little convenience store.

Holy cow.

What have I got myself into?

I shake my head to clear the cobwebs. The whole drive back from the harbor is a blur. All I could think about was her sitting next to me in that little white bikini.

And without that little white bikini.

It's her perfume. It's driving me crazy. What's under—

I slap my cheek. *Get it together, dude. You're a gentleman, remember?*

New Me growls, "Maybe not."

I flee to the bathroom and splash water on my face. Hands clamped on either side of the sink, I regard my reflection.

My pupils are wide, too wide. My cheeks are flushed. Stubble on my jawline. I meant to shave again before dinner.

I meant to do a lot of things.

I sweep my hair back into my Wall Street look.

Pit check. Not bad, not good. Wish I had some deodorant for a quick swipe.

I look myself in the eye and start a little pep talk.

Here's what's NOT going to happen—

1. I'm not going to take advantage of her.
2. I'm not going to act like a pig.
3. I'm not going to assume anything.
4. And I'm definitely not going to tell her something crazy like I love you before she has a chance to know me enough to love me back.

Okay. Now for a DO list—

1. I'm going to listen to her and get to know her better.
2. I'm going to make sure she gets home safely.
3. I'm going to talk to University of Hawaii's art school to see about teaching opportunities.
4. I'm going to call my landlord tomorrow and see about putting my stuff in storage.
5. I'm going to meet her family.
6. I'm going to marry Pua.

I look at the guy in the mirror and smile.
I like New Me.

JUSTIN & PUA

JUSTIN

I'm sitting on the table watching the last sliver of sun sink below the horizon when Pua returns carrying a plastic bag full of take out. I jump up and reach to take it from her, but she brushes past, steps off the pavilion, and onto the grass.

"Let's eat on the beach," she says.

"Sun's down," I say. "Sure you don't want to eat here?"

"I'm sure. The full moon is rising. Isn't it gorgeous?"

"You're gorgeous," I say.

"You didn't even look," she says.

I turn. Behind us, the moon is a pearl leaping from towering cliffs into the night sky. I watch as night closes in and the sky shines with the pinpricks of diamonds. I feel small and adrift in the vastness of the universe.

Yaddah, yaddah, yaddah.

I know that's the vibe she's going for, but I don't care.

I swivel back to her. "You're the only thing I want to see," I say.

"Food first. Let's head to the beach," she says. "It's private. We'll be away from the lights at the pavilion and Hari's store."

She turns and wanders down the hill, her hips swaying with every step.

I haven't moved, but I'm out of breath. Blood pounds in my head.

Remember the dos and don'ts.

Sasha appears in a housecoat and curlers. "You are so screwed," she says.

From your lips to God's ears, Sasha.

I take a deep breath and head to the beach. When I pass the shark sign, I jump and slap it for luck.

Pua

At the edge of the lava outcrop that leads to Piko Point, Pua slips off the sarong and spreads it out on the sand.

Her body is thrumming; she's certain if she's not careful sparks will fly from her fingers.

She sends her Niuhi senses out into the night.

The beach is empty from Nalupuki all the way to the pavilion.

Not even that mettlesome dog is around.

Perfect.

She unpacks food containers and cans of juice,

feeling Justin's approach through vibrations in the sand. She'll have to ask her questions quickly.

She knows the middle.

It's just the end that's uncertain.

It's also why her dinner is light.

She has no idea if she's eating dessert.

JUSTIN

It's dark on the beach. I hesitate for a second, but then I catch a glimpse of a white bikini smiling like teeth in the darkness.

"Pua?"

"Over here."

"Ah, using your sarong as a picnic blanket. Nice."

"Some things are better without sand," she says, handing me a plate.

"What's this? Smells delicious."

"Teri beef, rice, macaroni salad. More guava-passion fruit juice, too. Typical man food."

"Man food? What are you eating?"

"Fresh ahi sashimi and a little tako poke."

"What?"

"Sliced raw tuna and a salad of octopus and seaweed. Want some?"

She holds out her chopsticks.

I hear the challenge in her voice.

In the moonlight, the thin sliver of tuna glows like a ruby.

"Sure," I say. "I'm not afraid of a little raw fish."

She brings it to my lips. I open my mouth, and she places it like a communion wafer on my tongue.

It's refrigerator cold. I hold it in my mouth for a second, warming it back to life. I expect salt, I expect slime, but what I taste is sweet. Tentatively, I chew. The meat is tender, almost melting in my mouth.

I groan.

"More?" she teases.

"Yes."

"Too bad. It's gone. All that's left is man food."

"What? How did you eat it so fast?"

"Practice," she says.

PUA

He's a little clumsy with the chopsticks, but not too bad. He manages to get rice and beef into his mouth, with the occasional morsel of macaroni and mayonnaise thrown in. She waits until his blood pressure stabilizes, when his heartbeat slows and his mind relaxes, before she circles with her opening move.

JUSTIN

Pua says, "I know you're from California and an artist, but that's all I know."

I look up from my plate. "We really haven't talked about ourselves much, have we? I was born and bred in Garden Grove, California, and I'm finishing my MFA at UCLA. Only child, no siblings. You?"

"I have a twin brother, Kalei."

"A twin? Really? I'd love to meet him sometime."

She laughs. "I don't know about that."

"He doesn't like your *boyfriends*?"

I hold my breath.

"That's putting it mildly."

Boyfriend. She let that slide.

Score!

Sasha looks up from a magazine. "Desperate, much?"

For someone so in love with their soulmate Palo, you sure spend a lot of time in my head.

Sasha sniffs and turns a page.

"—in Hawaii?"

Crap. I missed that.

"It's complicated," I say.

PUA

"Do you know anyone in Hawaii?" Pua asks, stifling a burp. *A little too much chili in the poke,* she thinks

"It's complicated," Justin says.

Pua leans forward. It's the moment when a fish either turns and runs or gives up and presents its belly.

She likes offerings, but it's more fun to chase.

"I was engaged."

Horrified, Pua recoils. "To someone in Hawaii?"

Justin reaches for her hand. "No, no, nothing like that. Sasha and I were together for five years. We met at UCLA. She was a barista at the student union. We were planning our wedding. This trip was supposed to be our honeymoon, but she…changed plans, including the groom. Everything was non-refundable, so…" He shrugs.

Pua's eyes light up. "You came alone? What about your family or friends? Surely someone—"

Justin shakes his head. "There's no one. Over the years, Sasha kept me close. I didn't realize it until after she left that all my friends had gone, too. I haven't seen my best friend in years."

"What about family?"

"Gone, too."

"You're all alone in the world, aren't you, Justin?"

Pua stands in the moonlight as it bleeds into the ocean. The only sound is the lapping of waves along the shore. She hooks her thumbs into her bikini bottoms and shimmies.

"I can help with that," she says.

JUSTIN

My mouth drops to my chest; my lungs fill with her scent of sandalwood and salt. She drops to her knees and tugs my shirt over my head. Her lips brush mine, and it's like connecting with a live wire. Every nerve in my body lights up.

"Pua—"

She pulls her lips away and replaces them with her fingers. "Shhhhh. You talk too much." She takes my hand and places it on her breast.

"Pua—"

"Shhhh," she breathes, and her breath is dark and deep as the ocean.

She slips her fingers under my waistband and tugs.

I break all my rules.

PUA

She was right.

Gratitude.

What she didn't expect was how thoroughly he scratched her itch.

Maybe she'll visit him in California.

She could use a pet like him.

Nestled against his chest, she counts his breaths, one for every two waves that roll onshore. The moon has passed its zenith. In a few hours it will follow the sun over the horizon. It's the time of night when humans sleep.

And others walk.

She should leave him here and walk into the ocean.

Easier that way.

She starts to stand when something crunches underfoot. She reaches down and pulls a ki leaf lei from his pants pocket.

Oh, no. Oh, son of a sea serpent, no!

"Justin," she urges. "Wake up."

"Wha—?" He blinks, reaching for her. "What's wrong?"

"Why do you have this?" she says, waving the lei in his face.

He takes it from her, squinting. "Oh. A kid gave it to

me." He laughs. "Said it would protect me from sharks."

She shakes his shoulder. "Why would a local kid give a ki leaf lei to a tourist?"

"He said it was because I was a Coconut."

"What does that mean?"

"Brown on the outside, white on the inside. I grew up in Orange County, but my mom's family's originally from Lauele."

Pua goes still as stone.

"Is there any more juice?" Justin asks. "I'm so thirsty."

Pua places her hand on her abdomen. Two faint points of light flicker, but aren't whole yet.

There's time.

"I can't believe I fell asleep," says Justin. "How can I make it up to you?"

Pua says, "A midnight swim makes everything better."

JUSTIN

Pua grabs my hands and pulls me to my feet. I reach for her, but she dances away. In two seconds, she's knee-deep in the waves.

"C'mon," she calls. "The water flows like silk."

I walk to the edge where sea-foam nibbles my toes.

"I thought islanders didn't swim at night?" I say.

"Scaredy-cat," she says. "What could possibly hurt you here?"

She wades deeper and dives under a wave, stroking out until she's treading water.

Still holding the lei, I walk out until I'm knee-deep.

"Are you sure about this?"

She comes back and takes my hand, water cascading down her body. "More sure now than ever, Justin. Come join me in the water." She sees the lei and twitches. "Get rid of that rotten thing. You're mine now."

14

JUSTIN & PUA

JUSTIN

The ocean's different at night.

Pua guides me past the shore break and out to where the waves roll like a rocking chair. It's peaceful cradled in darkness. For the first time in a long time, I look at the sky and know my place in the universe.

"You were right," I say. "A swim is exactly what we need."

Pua side-strokes to my left.

I have to spin in the water to follow her.

I laugh. "This reminds me of a game we used to play: Marco Polo."

"I know it," she says and dives beneath the surface.

"Marco," I say.

I hear her come up behind me. "Polo," she says.

Water is tricky. Echoes bounce and distort distances.

I know she can't be more than an arm's length behind me, but her voice comes as if she's twenty yards to sea.

Something splashes to my right. I spin toward it.

"Marco?"

Something cold brushes against my back.

"Polo," she whispers in my ear. Her arm snakes around from behind, and I feel her body spoon against mine. As she releases me, she trails a nail across my chest.

In the darkness, I shiver. I can't tell the sea from the sky. Every hair on my body stands at attention.

"You're good," I say.

She leans forward and kisses the nape of my neck, sending a pulse of energy down my spine.

She nudges me in the small of my back, and then she's gone again.

Is that her to the left?

"Marco?"

Treading water, something sweeps against my toes.

I feel her break the surface and circle to my right.

"It's so dark out here, I can't see you." I pause. "Maybe it's better this way."

PUA

They're out too far for Justin to scramble for shore, too far for anyone walking the beach to see or hear, even if anyone cared to look. The tide is heading out. If she's careful, not even blood will make it to shore.

In her womb, two sparks sputter. Twins. It's always twins.

He has no one. The most anyone will find is his rental car in the parking lot. Kahana and others may suspect, but no one will know for sure, and that way the shark hunts won't start up again.

Sharks eating humans create bounties. Bounties bring hooks and boats and leave blood dripping onto the docks from the mouths of innocent tiger, bull, and hammerhead sharks. Bounties and hunts bring photographs of shark bodies lining the docks in newspaper articles.

It brings fear and hysteria.

It's an endless cycle.

He's just a tourist, Pua thinks. *No one will even notice he's gone.*

Justin says, "Maybe it's better this way—in the darkness, I mean. You can't see my face. I don't want to scare you away, Pua."

As if.

"But I'm moving to Hawaii."

She pauses in the water, wary.

"I know you think this is sudden, but there's nothing for me in Cali. I've come alive here."

And now you're going to die.

Good-bye, Justin.

Good-bye, little sparks. You were dead before you were ever conceived.

But Pua flips on her back and floats, listening to his voice and hearing the truth behind his words.

"In Hawaii, I've discovered my purpose—I can create art here that changes the way people see the ocean. Thousands of people come to these islands. Just think of the impact my art will have on the world."

"You're deluding yourself," Pua says, gliding behind him.

Thigh or jugular?

Jugular.

That way he can't scream.

"No," he says. "Art moves people. If people care about the ocean, they'll stop polluting it. What we care about, we protect."

"You're one person out of billions," Pua says. "Why bother?"

"Because I love this place. I wish my family had never left. I wish we'd grown up together boogie boarding, going to prom, and watching the submarine races at Piko Point."

If we had, you would have known better when you saw me sleeping on the sand.

But I would've known you, too.

He sighs. "It's easier to talk this way in the dark when I can't see how ridiculous this sounds to you. I want you to know you've changed me, Pua. You're fearless."

"No one's fearless, Justin. We all have fathers."

"I don't believe you. You truly are fearless, Pua. You don't need me. You don't need anyone. You don't care about fancy cars or restaurants. A castoff sarong or a designer dress—it's all the same to you. You move through the world doing what you want, when you want. You give champagne to a girl because you know it will make her happy even though she's too young. You don't have a phone or a car because things always work out for you in *the usual way*. The rules don't apply to you because you make your own rules."

I'm Niuhi.

I take what I want and make my own rules.

Pua cups a hand over her belly.

And what I want is you.

"And that's what I've come to love," Justin says.

She jerks, startled.

"Love?" she says.

Justin sweeps a hand across his face. "I know, I know. It's too soon. You think it's the tropical night with the stars overhead, sex on the beach—it's out of some movie script, right?"

"I—" She fills her lungs and dives.

"Pua?"

Kalei will kill Justin.

Kalei will kill me.

Father will kill us both if Kalei tries to protect me.

Twins. One is bound to be a boy, the other a girl.

The boy I'll have to kill. But the girl—

The girl I will keep for my own.

I will be a mother.

She skims along the bottom, watching Justin's fluttering feet above.

He's a risk.

He needs to disappear.

One bump, then bite.

She spirals to the surface.

JUSTIN

I'm tired. Treading water is exhausting.

Pua's head rises from the water sleek as a seal.

Pua's not winded at all.

"Pua? Say something. Anything."

"I don't have the words," she says.

I lick my lips and taste salt.

I say, "I promised myself I wouldn't do this, Pua, that I would go slow and give you time to get to know me, to know us, before saying I love you."

"Do you always keep your promises?"

"Yes."

She splashes me. "That's a lie. You just told me you broke promises you made to yourself when you said you love me."

"You misunderstood. To tell you I love you is not a lie or a broken promise. It's the truth. My word is my bond, Pua. If I promise you something, I will die before breaking it."

"And your debts?"

"I pay them. All of them."

PUA

The konane board shifts and the stones realign to reveal another option.

Pua spots it immediately,

It's risky, so risky, she thinks. *It will only work if I can hide my son in plain sight. No one can know he is Niuhi. Kalei cannot suspect my son even exists. But then Father can't hold Kalei accountable for what he doesn't know.*

If this works, we'll be safe from the punishment of death for breaking kapu.

Kahana and that blasted dog 'Ilima will have to help.

And Justin will have to go and never come back or it all falls apart.

I can't have him recognizing himself in a son or chasing after me because he thinks he's in love.

But maybe, just maybe, if both twins are to live, he doesn't have to die.

JUSTIN

Like a ship coming out of fog bank, Pua emerges from the darkness. She wraps her arms around my neck, her legs around my waist. With her body tangled in mine, it should be harder to stay at the surface, but she's buoyant.

For once I'm not struggling in the water.

She places her forehead against mine and leans forward so our noses touch. I breathe in her breath, and it's like sunshine, lemons, and sandalwood.

"Konane," she says. "Do you remember it?"

"Of course," I say.

"The reason you lost at konane is because you think the game is all about devouring your opponent's pieces. It's not. It's about keeping your own options open and always having another move to make."

She swivels her head, rubbing her nose against mine once, twice.

"Eskimo kisses," I say.

"You owe me, Justin," she says. "There's a debt that's due."

I laugh. "The gambling debt? Do you know what you want?"

She nods and captures my mouth. Images of waves fill my mind; castles of coral rise from the deep; I hear chanting and drums as shadows dance in firelight.

She kisses and kisses until all the oxygen is gone from my body.

I begin to faint.

Darkness rolls like deep sea breakers on their way to shore.

I feel heavy and weak as a newborn pup.

I start to sink.

She pulls back and breathes life into my nostrils.

My eyes are open, but I see nothing, not even stars.

"Justin," she says. "I am not free. I can never be yours. You must swear on the debt you owe me that you will leave these islands and never, ever come back."

"What?" I'm so dizzy, my chin sinks below surface and water fills my mouth. "No!" I sputter.

"Swear it!"

"No."

She grabs my shoulders and pushes my head underwater.

She holds.

And holds.

I struggle.

She holds.

A light appears behind my eyelids. I feel my spirit rise and rush toward it like a bullet train through a tunnel.

Still she holds.

This is how I die.

I'm suddenly stone-cold sober and thinking clearly.

This girl is nucking-futz.

She's cray-cray Loonie Tunes.

She's going to kill me, and there's nothing I can do about it.

I'm no longer struggling when she pulls my head out of the water.

"Swear," she says.

"I swear," I say. "Just please let me go. I'll never come back."

Pua brushes her lips against mine. "Aloha, Justin," she says. "Remember your promise. Never come back. If you do, you've murdered us all."

She releases me and disappears into the night.

15

EPILOGUE

JUSTIN

When I make it back to shore, the first thing I do is throw up. The second is gather my things and climb into the car. The concierge doesn't bat an eye when I stagger into the lobby, trailing sand and a broken heart.

He's a pro. It's just another day in paradise, right? It's like the captain said: it all looks different in the morning.

I'm just another tourist who fell victim to a local psycho.

Who doesn't have a phone or car?

Who won't tell me where she lives?

Who sleeps on the beach in the afternoon?

Mental patient escapees, that's who.

Why didn't I see it sooner?

Did she put something in my drink?

Did I get roofied?

From the honeymoon suite, I call the airline and change my ticket for the next flight back to California. I shower, throw my stuff in a bag, and get the hell out of Dodge.

Wheels up on the runway, I order a Coke, dump in some rum, and pull out my sketchbook.

Pua, asleep on the beach.

Why? Why do I always attract the crazy?

In the empty window seat, imaginary Pua tucks her hair behind her ear.

"I said I wasn't free, not that I didn't love you, Justin."

You're telling me you're a prisoner? Of what, like the mob? Is your father part of the Yakuza? Is that what you meant when you said he allowed aquariums? Were you really trying to protect me by making me leave?

Pua smiles without showing her teeth. "Oh, Justin," she says, "We're going to have so much fun."

PUA

She swims to the arch at Piko Point where she rests in the big saltwater pool until daylight brightens the sky. For the first time in a week, the infernal itching is gone from under her dorsal fin.

Too bad she can never have Justin scratch that itch again.

Boy had talent.

The sparks in her womb are lively.

Hungry.

That little bit of sashimi and poke on the beach were never going to be enough.

She smacks her lips, considering.

Something warm and fatty. A dolphin or a seal? I'll head to the northern islands and hunt. Maybe visit Aunty Ake. She'll help me figure out how to hide a male child I cannot raise in plain sight.

Two shakes of her mighty tail send her out into the channel.

She doesn't look back to see the octopus slithering out of his hiding place.

KANALOA

The great ocean god Kanaloa smiles.
Things are going just as he planned.

Justin and Pua's story continues in
One Boy, No Water,
Book 1 of the Niuhi Shark Saga trilogy.

TALKING STORY NEWSLETTER

Want to receive free bonus content, sneak peeks, special event announcements, writing tips from the Lehua Writing Academy, and exclusive perks on upcoming titles from Makena Press? Sign up for Lehua Parker's Talking Story Newsletter. You can change your subscription preferences at anytime. New subscribers get an exclusive welcome bonus.

Subscribe to
Talking Story Newsletter

http://www.lehuaparker.com/newsletter

ABOUT LEHUA PARKER

LEHUA PARKER writes speculative fiction for kids and adults that often explores the intersections of Hawaii's past, present, and future. Her published works in the Lauele Universe include the Niuhi Shark Saga trilogy, Lauele Chicken Skin Stories, and Lauele Fractured Folktales, as well as plays, poetry, short stories, and essays.

As an author, editor, and educator trained in literary criticism and advocate of indigenous cultural narratives, Lehua is a frequent presenter at conferences, symposiums, and schools. Her hands-on workshops and presentations for kids and adults are offered through the Lehua Writing Academy.

Originally from Hawai'i and a Kamehameha Schools graduate, Lehua now lives in exile in the Rocky Mountains. During the snowy winters, she dreams of the beach.

Connect with her at:

www.LehuaParker.com

Subscribe to Talking Story Newsletter at
www.LehuaParker.com/newsletter